YEARS

Celebrating 50 Years

Mercier Press is the oldest independent Irish
publishing house and has published books in the
fields of history, literature, folklore, music, art,
humour, drama, politics, current affairs, law
and religion. It was founded in 1944 by John
and Mary Feehan.

In the building up of a country
few needs are as great as that of a publishing
house which would make the people proud of
their past, and proud of themselves as a people
capable of inspiring and supporting a world of
books which was their very own. Mercier Press
has tried to be that publishing house. On the
occasion of our fiftieth anniversary we thank
the many writers and readers who have
supported us and contributed to our success.

We and half-century
e.

PRIZE-WINNING RADIO STORIES

INTRODUCTION

by

MICHAEL LITTLETON

Published in association with
Radio Telefís Éireann

MERCIER PRESS

Mercier Press
PO Box 5, 5 French Church Street, Cork
24 Lower Abbey Street, Dublin 1

© Contributors

ISBN 1 85635 081 9

A CIP is available of this book from the British Library

Printed in Ireland by Colour Books.

Contents

Introduction by Michael Littleton   7

Wire me to the Moon: *Margaret Dolan*   11

Forecourt: *Katy Hayes*   17

When it Got Serious: *Ronan Brady*   22

My Mother's Daughter: *Ivy Bannister*   27

The Blind Arch: *Michael Coady*   33

Behind Glass (*or* My Life with Bishop Berkeley):
    Pat Boran   38

The Lost Citadel: *Mary O'Donnell*   44

Billy in the Summer of 1962: *Aodhan Madden*   49

Tompkins Square Park: *Margaret Dolan*   55

The Dancing Chicken of Chinatown: *Ivy Bannister*   61

The Suit: *Pat Boran*   67

Everybody's Gone: *Martin Meenan*   73

Sentimental Reasons: *Máiríde Woods*   78

African Sanctus: *Marie Hurley*   84

Blood Relations: *Ivy Bannister*   91

I Do Love You Rita Kelly: *Max McGowan*   97

Olly: *Michael Tubridy*   103

The Illusionist: *Tom Duddy*   109

The Skull Beneath the Skin: *Barbara McKeon*   116

The Last Butterfly: *Alan Titley*   121

Wasps: *Joe O'Donnell*   127

Nicaraguan Coffee: *Joe O'Donnell*   133

Allegiance: *Maura Treacy*   139

An International Incident: *Emma Cooke*   145

Barney, Ellie, Des and the Couple in the Car:

    Joe O'Donnell   151

And the Street went Blind: *Pat Boran*   158

The Clear Night of Day: *Michael Coady*   165

A Change in the Weather: *Ciarán Ó Cualáin*   170

A Ribbon of Rainbow: *Eoin Ó Laighin*   176

Esther: *Ursula de Brún*   182

Nothing Changes Except the Water: *Peter Hutchinson*   188

The Coast of Malabar: *John Maher*   194

Introduction

'The MacManus'

People mostly called him Frank because that was how he preferred to be addressed. Behind his back, however, they tended to refer to him as Mr MacManus. Even after more than three decades, I have known no other individual in broadcasting who commanded so strong a sense of affection and respect as the man, in honour of whose memory, RTE Radio One has named its annual short story competition.

Francis MacManus was himself a writer of renown whose published work forms a distinctive component of Irish literary output in the first half of the twentieth century. Indeed, it is still a feature of the school curriculum. However, it was as a broadcasting organiser – in effect he was Radio Éireann's literary and features editor – that he reached his widest audience.

The range of his professional activity was extraordinary by present day standards. He was responsible for religious broadcasting, agricultural and gardening programmes, public affairs and topical series, Irish language programming, film and book reviewing, as well as stories, poetry and other literary features. He also introduced regular coverage of national and international affairs – forerunners to the current affairs programmes of today. Both in terms of breadth of interest and a sense of excellence in practice, his is an enduring legacy, still at the heart of public service radio in the 1990s.

The Thomas Davis Lectures remain the best known radio monument to his work and to his ideals. Introduced in autumn 1953 – and called after Thomas Davis because of his saying 'Educate that you may be free' – this new departure was designed to bring to a wider non-specialist public, the best available Irish scholarship in popular form. History, Literature, Economics, Social Life, Geography, Politics, Religion, Trade Unionism, were just some of the vast number of subject areas covered. As most of the series found their way into print subsequently, (the majority published by Mercier Press) there was a permanent record developed and available to listeners and the general public at a reasonable price because it was Frank's policy to concentrate on paperback publication.

Later, in his history of the formative years of this development, Professor F X Martin was to comment (Irish *Historical Studies*, Vol XV, No 59, March 1967): 'The name of Francis MacManus, the general features officer, is inseparable from the Thomas Davis lectures ... He became in fact the director of the Thomas Davis Lectures and was the element of continuity from one session to another. He stood in no awe of intellectuals, since he himself was a writer of distinction, with an intimate sense of Irish tradition and a rounded knowledge of several European literatures. He proposed new series, he selected consulting editors, he contacted likely lecturers, and cajoled or convinced them into agreement. This was only half the work. He had to ensure that the scripts would be ready on time, and then to read, assess and, if necessary, prune them without offending the susceptibilities of the authors. All this he did with energy, a puckish sense of humour, and an idealist's dedication to his work.' Today, forty years since their foundation, and twenty-eight years since his premature death on 27 November 1965, the Thomas Davis Lectures continue to be broadcast and published along the lines he originated so long ago.

As a man he made a strong impact on all who knew and worked with him. He had high standards and was extremely demanding of himself and others. I worked as his assistant for five years and can bear testimony to his driving interest in his work, executed with a powerful flair for the dramatic, and leavened by a wicked sense of humour. To one famous author (who believed his work was being rejected without full consideration) he wrote ... 'I am returning your script which is not up to your best standard. I do not believe that I would change this judgment even if I could read page 6, which you have glued – inadvertantly no doubt – to the back of page 5.' To another famous man of letters he gave the shortest reply to the longest letter I have ever seen – an eighteen page denunciamento full of complaints and demands: 'Dear –, No. Yours sincerely, Francis MacManus'.

Day-to-day working life was for him an endless running battle with contributors who were – he was convinced – constantly on the brink of letting him down. He pursued them relentlessly. Some pretended to leave the country to avoid him – one or two actually did so – all to no avail because his reach was long indeed, and he never gave up.

Sometimes stronger measures were needed. Once he sacked a reviewer who had failed to meet three successive deadlines. An hour later he was in my office with an elaborate conspiracy fully prepared. I was to go after the delinquent, sympathise with him and offer to slip him back into the programme under a false name without Frank knowing ... This charade produced many years of excellent, reliable contributions.

This, then, is something of a flavour of the man after whom the short story competition is named, kind and considerate despite a frenetic work style and one who never allowed the burdens of personal and family ill-health become a factor in his dealings with others. In 1985 we marked the twentieth anniversary of his death, by broadcasting a series of Thomas Davis Lectures about his life and work. In the following year because of dearth of both quantity and quality in submitted scripts, we decided to try the effect of a public competition and were somewhat taken aback to receive about 1,000 entries. Bearing in mind that these are crafted pieces of almost 2,000 words in length, this was an astonishingly high level of response. Even more astonishingly, this rate of entry has remained the average in the eight years over which the competition has run so far.

Each year there are four prizes on offer – £1,000 and a trophy for the overall winner and runners-up prizes of £500, £300 and £200. Just as important, perhaps, is the fact that RTE Radio 1 broadcasts not just the winning stories but an entire season selected from among the best of the other entries. This offers real possibilities of encouragement to aspiring writers and some have gone on to develop careers in writing as a result of having had a crack at 'the MacManus'.

In the 1993 competition, Mercier Press entered the field with a special additional prize of £1,000. This was a public gesture to mark the forthcoming Golden Jubilee year of their foundation and is particularly appropriate because of the close ties in publishing between their founder, Seán Feehan and Francis MacManus of Radio Éireann, as it then was known. In the same spirit, they offered to publish the prize-winning stories to date in a single volume – and here they are.

I should like, on behalf of RTE, to thank each of the authors for their co-operation in this venture. I want to acknowledge with real appreciation the work of the producers at the core of the preliminary selection process, Seamus Hosey and Kate Minogue, as well as that of Padraic O'Neill, who also chairs the final judging stage. I want to remember also the part played in this for so many years by the late producer, Maxwell Sweeney. Above all, perhaps, RTE owes a debt of gratitude to the many distinguished writers, critics and academics who have served as judges for the competition with so generous a disregard for the pressures on their own time. Finally, I would like to think that there may yet be a Volume Two out of it all soon into the next century.

MICHAEL LITTLETON
Features Editor, RTE Radio 1
and General Editor, Thomas Davis Lectures.

Wire me to the Moon

Margaret Dolan

This morning sun entered my body. It came streaming in through the window, through the blinds in gold bars spreading hope, wrapping me in its warm glow.

When the sun hit the prism, colours spiralled around me like I was inside a spinning top. Rainbow colours. Happy colours. I hugged myself with the unbearable thrill of being alive.

After the operation, after they sliced off half my left breast I was immersed in a maelstrom of turbulent dark and malevolent colours swirling around inside me. Muddy browns and maroons, greens and purples. Mostly the colour purple. One big purple pain scorching through my body on a scream.

For a while I drifted on a grey fog of drugs keeping pain at bay. But even then a huge blot of yellow, cowardice yellow would whoosh through me. Terrifying me into childhood prayers. If I'd been x-rayed at that time my whole inside would have been one great big splodge of cowardly yellow.

But right now, at this very minute on this light and upbeat golden day ... I'm pure gold. The sun has entered my body and I have the Midas touch.

I want to spread the news, spread the good word. Tell Jean.

One day, one ordinary day you wake and there it is. Surprise, surprise. Waiting to be discovered. Fright creeps up your neck like a hot hand. Your eyes run down your face to the spot. Not wanting to see what your fingers feel. A cluster, like spring bulbs or seeds that bump up the earth ready to burst through. Only these are not expected, not sown by me. The Judas kiss of cancer planted in my breast.

Mastectomy skitters around my head in lumps. Lump, tumour, growth. A lump by any other name ... oh God ... oh

11

God ...

A month after the operation when the wound had healed I was wired up. Through my left breast ... New treatment ... sealing, killing off cells.

'Wire me to the moon,' I say half laughing to the young nurse. She half laughed too.

'I could light up like a Christmas tree,' I say.

Blue. Radio-active stuff pumped through my breast on wires. To gobble up aspiring lumps. Emptying my left breast.

I want Jean. I want my sister more than anything else. If she knew, she would drop everything and fly half way round the world to be with me. That's why I didn't tell her.

I want to tell someone though, anyone and everyone what it was like. Especially Cora.

Cora who doesn't want to know.

Cora who wants to know everything else ...

Cora who has pinned me to the cabbages beside the deep freeze in the supermarket extracting information from me. Gossip. Information I didn't want to give. Shouldn't have given.

Hurtful, sad information.

I, the only one with the information. I held back the news from Breda and Nora but I told Cora Malone.

The three of them, Cora, Breda and Nora were off playing golf and missed the drama of the runaway wife.

Breda and Nora came the following day sniffing around with their cream cake and sly looks. Hunting information. Asking questions. They knew she had flown. There had been talk. It had been expected. Her wings had been flapping for some time. But they were truly miffed to miss the flight. And on their doorstep too.

Did she time it deliberately to vex them? No, she wouldn't have given them a thought.

So having missed the big picture they came for the details. The nitty gritty. I made coffee.

'You must have seen,' they said. 'The afternoon ... you always garden in the afternoon.'

I could feel the tic in my right eye racing with lies as I

denied seeing what I had seen.

From the herbaceous border I witnessed Sonia Kennedy leaving her husband and watched him literally crawl down the path after her, begging, beseeching. Saw her jump into her lover's jeep and zoom away. Her pony tail bobbing. I was the only, on-the-spot witness apart from their three little blonde girls.

'Get up, get up,' the eldest, ten year old Florence ordered her father, in her mother's clipped tone. 'You're making an exhibition of yourself.'

The middle child said nothing just rolled her hands into tiny fists. The youngest sucked her thumb vigorously.

Cora got me in the supermarket between the cabbages and the deep freeze cornering me with her trolley.

I still said I saw nothing ... then after much interrogating I said nothing-much ...

And then with my knee hopping with held back information and my eye ticking, she extracted every single bit from me. Bits I didn't remember seeing ... The whole bloody scene like a scab lifting. The humiliating scene with poor Peter begging on his knees.

And I felt guilty and miserable. So much so that I began bringing around cakes and things to the Kennedy family and offering to help. Peter was mortified. Looked away. The eldest resented me being a witness too. The middle one didn't seem to care and the little one slid her hand in mine and her little warm hand made me want to cry.

I didn't let them down any more but it didn't change anything. I had betrayed them to the mob. Held their pain up to ridicule. Gave it to Cora beside the cabbages in the supermarket. She glowed, hardly able to contain herself. She had it straight from the eejit's mouth. She could hold forth in the golf club. Holding every eye and ear with each juicy morsel. Embroidering as well of course. Maybe even have the jeep running over his fingers and by the time the story left the club, Peter would be in intensive care with multiple injuries.

I knew it couldn't get back to him. He didn't go out any more. Better if it did. He could accuse me. I could admit, apologise, ask forgiveness.

What he couldn't forgive me for, was being there, witnessing.

When the removal van came they drove after it without looking at me in my herbaceous border, except for a tiny wave from the little one. I felt justly punished.

Cora seldom cornered me after that in the supermarket, I was no use to her. Except as a listener to her aches and pains. She told me about her hysterectomy, from diagnosis to operation, to after-effects. Every stitch. The lot. Nobody had suffered like she had. And everyone, just everyone said how brave she was. Even got a holiday in Barbados for her bravery.

The nurses said I was brave. 'A model of courage,' they said. I wasn't of course. But I grabbed the lie anyway and held on to it. I was afraid, afraid of death but mostly afraid of pain. I wanted them to knock me out, anaesthetise me, stuff me full of pain-killers and valium. Or at least hit me on the head with a mallet.

'A little tug and that'll be it. Won't feel a thing ... well, maybe a teeny tiny prick like a prick of a needle,' the doctor said.

Nobody thought the wires would stick. That the flesh would grow over them. I didn't want to be there in my blue radio-active room, in my senses watching and feeling the wires stick.

'Get a grip,' the doctor says when I start to whimper.

I can see his dandruff ... smell his breath, his sweat.

'Good girl,' he says when I stop.

He pulls. I want to scream my pain to the world.

A tiny little moan sneaks out of the corner of my mouth.

'You're not helping,' he says.

Helping? Helping who?

He who said I didn't need a local anaesthetic.

He who hasn't got a breast with lumps and wires stuck in it. He who doesn't care, wants to pull the wire out of me with my flesh attached.

He who now says I'm not helping.

This guinea pig squeals long and loud and full of pain.

Showing him up.

He wants to slap me. I want to kick him to death.

'SISSSSS ...' involuntarily waters through the nurses' teeth as they watch.

When the wires came out harbouring bits of my flesh he couldn't look me in the eye. Sister gave me pain-killers and brandy and I slept and slept.

The whistle blows. I've got it. The all clear. They've let me out. I want to howl it to the skies. Or at least from the bean-stack in the supermarket. I want to stand on the pile of bean tins and scream, 'I'm all right. They've taken it away.'

Along with bits of me of course.

Breda, Nora and Cora are in the supermarket. They see me coming. Pushing my trolley. Breda nudges Nora at the wines and nods in my direction. Surprised I am alive and well and shopping. Embarrassed. Probably informed the golf club the neighbourhood spinster had IT, the big C ... and whispered 'it's only a matter of time'.

Breda is preparing to bolt with her wire basket.

'How are you,' she shouts on the hoof as I wheel my trolley towards her, dashing past before I can say 'Fine, I'm fine' or better still, 'Rumours of my death have been greatly exaggerated'. But she is gone.

'How is everything?' Nora says when I catch up with her at confectionery. Eyes fastened on the cream doughnuts.

'Examine yourself,' I say sowing the seeds of fear. 'It's everywhere.' She takes off, scalded by my words. God forgive me but I'm glad, really glad.

Cora actually abandoned her groceries and left the supermarket rather than meet me.

Nobody wants to press me up against the freezer and extract the details from me. The word is enough to make them run for cover. I don't need a leper's bell.

If I'd a bypass they'd have come around, settled down, made themselves comfortable wanting to know everything. Ask about the veins. Ask to see the wound. Asked about the diet. Count the stitches. Might even have visited me in hospital.

But they don't want to know about my mastectomy.

I wanted to tell them about that. I want to be told again I was a model of courage.

I wanted to tell them, Breda, Nora and Cora, the wires didn't come out clean. They stuck, like a chicken on a rotisserie. Bits of flesh, my flesh left on the wires.

I wanted to tell Cora especially. To pin her to the deep freeze, watch her turn green. Unburden myself. Off-load my pain. Freeze her blood.

Through the glass doors I watch Cora, running scared across the car park. Tomorrow, or the next day I'll follow her here. Ram her trolley, stick her to the freezer and tell her everything. Everything she doesn't want to hear.

The sky is blue. Hopeful blue and the sun is shining. I can't wait to feel its warmth again treacling through me.

I'll write and tell Jean ... Start with the Midas touch and go on from there ...

Oh look ... there's a butterfly.

Forecourt

Katy Hayes

I arrive and the garage is sleeping quietly. I have it open and ready for business by six-thirty. I love my job. I got summer holidays on June the sixth, and started work here straight away. I'm only working on the petrol pumps. You have to be here six months before they allow you start being a mechanic. The manager is a friend of my older sister. She used to go out with him. He is very ugly. My sister's taste in men is fairly dreadful.

I always wear figure-hugging denims to work. They make my bum look nice. I can usually see out of the corner of my eye that all the mechanics are looking at me and my ass. When it's sunny like today, I wear a little vest top with bare arms and bare neck. I look at my reflection in the mirror. It's a bit clean looking, so I rub a bit of engine oil just over my right breast and on my cheek. It looks really cute. I got a new bra and it makes my boobs look great. It kind of raises them up a bit and points them outwards. Not like the boring yokes my Ma gets for me. Sports bras. They're made out of plain white stretchy cotton and they kind of flatten out your tits and tuck half of them under your armpits.

My mother is a feminist. She keeps talking about equality in the workplace, and she says there should be more women in male-dominated jobs. I thought she would be pleased that I had got a job as a petrol pump attendant, but I think she was thinking more in terms of brain surgery. My older sister Pam tells her not to be so bloody bourgeois. When Mary Robinson was up for the presidency my mam made all my brothers vote for her. She said there wouldn't be another hot dinner in our house unless that woman got into the Park. My brothers all joked and said they'd vote according to their conscience. My mother is their conscience. I am too young to vote but I would have voted for Mary Robinson if I could. I think she has great legs. When I'm as old as her I hope I look as good as her. Why can't my mam dress like her instead of wearing denims all the time? She doesn't have the figure for denims. I wish she'd dress her age.

I know all the regular customers. I have great chats with them. There's one man in particular. Colm Cronin is his name. I know 'cos it's written on his credit card. Lovely name. He drives a black BMW. He stares into my eyes as I hand him back his car keys, and winks at me before he drives out of the forecourt. When he asks me how I am, he seems to really want to know.

His missus is also gorgeous. She is like a model. Tall, blonde, lots of suntan. They have one kid, a little girl who is an absolute stunner. Long blonde curls, cute pout. The missus comes into me about as often as he does, but during the morning, on her way to do the shopping. She drives a bright red Toyota Starlet. Usually she doesn't pay me, but asks me to put her bill onto his when he comes in later on, and he pays for the lot with his credit card. I'm not really supposed to do that, but so far they haven't let me down, he's always made it in before the end of my shift, so the Boss can't possibly know that I do it.

Sometimes I imagine myself driving the Starlet. I look great in red. I drive home with my kid, I'd call her Saffron, to a beautiful house surrounded by trees, and I'd cook his dinner for him. Something posh out of me mam's cordon bleu book. Then he'd come home and fly into a jealous rage and throw the dinner on the floor, on account of him thinking that I'm having an affair with his business partner, but then he'd say he's sorry and couldn't help himself because he's so tormented with adoration for me. Then we'd slip into something more comfortable and lie in each other's arms listening to U2 singing 'All I Want is You', then we'd dive into bed and make glorious, amazing, mega-fabuloid love. No, we wouldn't get as far as the bed. We'd do it on the carpet. We'd devour each other with kisses and bites and eventually we'd do you know what, and afterwards we'd lie there panting.

Sometimes I feel a bit guilty when I see his wife. I

18

wonder has she any idea about me and him.

Though I like my job, it can be a little bit dull. I've figur-ed out a way to keep myself amused. If I position the pump nozzle in such a way while I'm filling the petrol tank, and hold my crotch against the tubing, the vibrations caused by the petrol flowing through makes me feel quite excited. It's a lovely tingly feeling. I could do it all day. Especially on a hot day.

As morning becomes midday I am getting hot and sweaty. I spend my time tidying and thinking about what the mechanics would look like with no clothes on. Colm's wife comes in. I fill her up and she smiles at me and tells me that he'll be up later to pay me. When she smiles she is a real smasher, but her eyes are slightly glazed and she doesn't really see me. Most of the customers are like that.

My big sister Pam and her current boyfriend Podge call in to me and try to scab some free petrol. I take off my sister's Ray Bans and hide them under the counter. She'd kill me if she knew I had them. They're real, not fake. She got them in New York. Podge is the ugliest boy in Dublin. He has chronic acne. He is twenty-three and he still has acne! I got a spot once, when I was thirteen. It lasted two weeks and then it went away. I haven't had one since. Puberty, I sup-pose. Podge's spots are really angry looking. I once asked Pam did she close her eyes when she kissed him and she didn't speak to me for two days. He drives a rusty heap of shit. Honestly, it is primitive. Pam, as always, is looking lovely in a gorgeous red and white polka dot mini dress. There is no point in Pamela dressing up when she has the Incredible Hulk on her arm. I've tried to tell Pam that it is embarrassing for me that she has gone out with every ugly guy in Dublin. She told me that pretty boys are crap in bed. In my opinion, it isn't a problem if they're ugly in bed, you could switch the lights out, it's just when they're out on the streets in public that they should be presentable. Besides, you spend much longer with them out of bed than in it. Podge pours his own petrol and makes funny faces in the window at Pam, who is laughing loudly. The two of them would have really ugly kids. Pamela coming here annoys me. This is my place. My sister never leaves me alone. No matter what I do she comes along and pokes her nose into it. I'm sick of her.

My kiosk is mostly made of glass so when it is as sunny as it is today it becomes incredibly hot. I try and stand in the shade a good bit, 'cos my shoulders are beginning to burn. The sun is baking down and the air is incredibly still, no breeze at all. I begin to sweat. Colm. Colm. I can't get his face out of my mind. He'll be up later. At half-past three I begin my end of shift routine. I start to count the cans of oil and add up the money. My till is going to be ten pounds short because he hasn't come in to pay for her petrol yet. Never mind, I'll explain to Bob, the three stone overweight boy who takes over from me at four. At a quarter to four I hear the unmistakable sound of Colm's engine. I am bent over my figures. As his car comes to a halt I look up and my insides leap. I go out to his car window and he hands me his keys, I see small beads of sweat on his temples and wet patches under his armpits. I can smell him. His eye is caught by the oil smear on my right breast. I colour unnoticeably under the screaming sun, and I feel blood rush to my groin. I open the petrol tank, put the pump nozzle in, and squeeze the trigger. The temptation is irresistible, so I slide my crotch over to it and a shiver goes down my back. I've never done it with his car before. I can feel my breath get faster. He switches on the car stereo and suddenly the air is filled with 'All I Want is You'. I look at the meter. It reads fifteen ninety-five and it's churning fast. The car holds twenty-six pounds usually. The petrol fumes rise to my nose as the sun beats down on the back of my neck and Bono's voice rings out across the forecourt. I pass a point and I cannot stop and suddenly I explode and a noise erupts from inside me, loudly. I hear myself groan like an animal, as the petrol tank overflows and petrol runs down my jeans. The pump shuts off automatically. I stand there for a moment, the nozzle in my right hand, dripping petrol on the concrete forecourt.

Auto-pilot takes over. I hang up the nozzle and walk to the car window. I am terrified of his face. He turns to look at me and his cheeks are as red as his wife's car, his expression astonished. I feel more weird than embarrassed. I feel like my body belongs to someone else. My right breast is still tingling.

I walk into the kiosk with his card and do out the credit slip. He follows me in to sign it. I can smell him really strong now. He is still staring at me with a bewildered look, though there is a small smile threatening at the corner of his mouth. I look at him, desperate. He puts away his card and goes to give me the usual one pound tip. In mid gesture he catches my crazy eye and goes scarlet, the colour of his wife's car. He drops the coin and I bend down and he bends down to pick it up. Our heads crash against each other and we both reel backwards, and my head spins. He asks me if I'm all right, the pound coin forgotten on the oily floor. I close my eyes and pretend to faint, and he steadies me. I fall against his chest and he has no choice but to put his arm around me.

There are two other cars on the forecourt, beeping furiously in the afternoon heat but I don't care. I am in his arms. I am in his terrified arms and I don't care.

When it Got Serious

Ronan Brady

Looking down at the men, bustling around among the animals in the mart, I used to wish I was born old like them. Like the big, red-faced cattle-dealer with the white hat who often stumbled through the gate. I could do things that mattered and people would listen to me. Our house and the hotel next door were the only three-storey buildings on this street and our bedroom was at the top. I came there most Wednesdays to watch the to-and-fro. In the summer, I'd catch blue-bottles in the gauze window-curtain.

I started coming there more often after Gran took sick. She lived with us and liked me to be around her, but that finished with her illness. Up till then she controlled things from an old seat in the corner from which she could also see the comings and goings on mart days. I could do no wrong in her eyes and my sisters could do little right. But this special treatment wasn't worth the trouble I got from Mary and Liz, from my mother and everyone else, because of it.

I knew Gran bothered my mother and that she was unfair to my sisters. But there wasn't much I could do about that, any more than I could do anything about the RUC men who loomed around our school at times, or Master Ferguson with his split cane. Gran often disagreed with my mother, especially about us. She was Da's mother, but he was out working most of the time and anyway, she *was* his mother.

Sometimes you could see Ma raging with her eyes when Gran contradicted her, although my mother never argued with the figure in the corner chair. I could recognise when Ma was angry because she'd start breathing very quickly. Then she'd suddenly leave the room with me and talk to the hat-stand downstairs as if it was an interfering old some-thing-or-other. After that she'd laugh.

Ma would take me upstairs to her room sometimes to teach me Irish or just to talk. There were all sorts of different words for things but what I really enjoyed was the fact that it was special, secret language, just between the two of us. She seemed younger than everyone else around and more lively. I think she liked dressing up in her uniform and going off to the hospital. She sometimes came home at odd times of the night and I'd catch her looking into our room after we'd gone to bed. Of course, I'd pretend to be asleep, so as not to worry her.

It was a quiet, quiet time, unlike now. The noisiest thing I remember is the sound of the trees in the park up behind our house. The slightest breath of wind would set their branches singing. There'd be weekends in Bundoran and once in a while we'd visit Ma's people in Loch an Iúir. It was funny crossing the border, you always felt you were a little bit more on holiday once you cleared the last customs post. The green post-boxes and the signs in Irish meant very little in themselves. But seeing them meant we'd left something slightly uncomfortable behind.

At school, we kept to our own and we had our own laughs. I remember when the RUC discovered an arms dump in a field two miles from the school. 'Somebody's up shit creek,' said the class comedian. 'Whoever let that be found is going to get a roasting,' and we laughed. The odd RUC barracks would get peppered from time to time, but it was all a bit of a romp. No one could take that very seriously.

I'm not sure when it did get serious. But it seems to me that Gran's death had something to do with it. Maybe it was one of those coincidences that make you a millionaire or kill you. But everything changed after that. It was a winter afternoon and we'd just come back from school when Gran got very bad. We were sent out to play among the wet leaves at the back. There were always wet leaves and I loved the heavy smell.

My two sisters and I were taken upstairs when they found Gran had stopped breathing. Mary started to cry and young Liz was about to follow. But I pointed out that Gran hadn't been too kind to them and maybe there wasn't much to cry about. Mary stopped and we stared out at the mart. I wasn't really that heartless about Gran. It was just I couldn't take the crying for no purpose.

Then I was called downstairs and the girls were put to bed. My mother dressed me in a suit and I was taken into the parlour. Huge adults stood around in crowds, either praying or drinking. In Gran's room and around the doorway, rosaries were going at full belt. Half curious, half afraid I made my way towards the room where she lay. Above my head, two adults (I was never sure who) had a discussion over whether I should be allowed to see the corpse. Eventually, the crowd parted slightly and curiosity drew me in.

There was a grey otherness about her skin even though you could see someone had used a lot of makeup and the rosary beads wrapped around her fingers looked far too tight. Dad was kneeling by the bed with his head bowed. His face looked very red. As I stood there, the hum of prayer seemed to die away and something sterner, more inescapable took over. The tall oaks and sycamores behind the house rustled louder as the wind rose. I felt very cold.

My mother descended upon the scene in a flurry, asking who'd left me into the room. Her argument was with other people, so I didn't bother to tell her I just went in of my own accord. I was hustled out of the room and given tea. I could see Ma talking to friends of hers from the hospital. Her eyes were red and there was a catch in her voice. It turned out I'd be going to my Uncle's house ten miles away for the night. Ma would drive me. There was no point in disturbing the two girls as they were asleep. Another relative offered to drive instead but Ma said she needed the fresh air.

She was breathing quickly as we went downstairs. This time she ignored the hat-stand but, when the car was slow to start, she told it that the interfering aul thing still had her claws into the children, even after her death. That sounded weird, but I didn't ask any questions. This time Ma certainly wasn't laughing. It had begun to bucket and it was hard to say whether it was raindrops or tears that made her cheeks wet.

We were only a few minutes out of town when we were flagged down by a torch, difficult to see in the driving rain.

My mother stopped slowly, turned off her lights and wound down the window. A gun-barrel entered the car with a breath of cold air. Behind it there was a face, half-hidden by the raised collar of a black overcoat.

'Your licence please,' said a shaky voice.

'You know me well Jim Sinclair. I delivered your elder sister. Take that gun out of here this minute!'

There was a pause as the rain hissed down on the car and the wipers swished it away. Another figure with a torch was further up the road.

'Your licence, please.' The voice seemed shakier still.

My mother sat, silent and frozen with anger. Her licence was in the purse, in the handbag, at my feet. But she stared straight ahead, daring the B Special to make the next move. The second figure suddenly shouted something and shone his torch at the car, dazzling us. The barrel of the gun shuddered slightly and a hand went up to rub rainwater off the half-hidden face. Suddenly I saw it for the first time. He was young enough to have been on our school football team.

The hand went back to the trigger.

'Your licence please, I'm serious.'

My mother bent down and took up her bag. Slowly she found the purse without looking. Still staring straight ahead, she handed the licence to the B Special. The gun vanished and a wet hand took the document for a moment before handing it back.

Another figure appeared at the window, almost pushing the first one aside. A smiling, wet, hearty face said: 'Nurse McGirr, if we'd only known it was you ...'

'You don't know my number-plate? I thought I saw you looking at it with your torch.'

'Ah, you're a good one, Nurse McGirr.' The hearty face laughed but the voice sounded very false. My mother abruptly rolled up her window and drove on.

I stared straight ahead for the rest of the journey and neither of us said anything. When we reached my Uncle's place, my mother rushed out and rang the bell. She was going to say something to my Aunt but instead she started crying and it was a long time before I was put to bed.

Things were different after Gran's death in ways I don't quite understand. The conversations with the hat-stand stopped completely, even when Ma was raging. The Irish lessons stopped as well, except for when we went to see Ma's family in the Rosses. I missed them even more than the one-sided chats with a piece of carved oak in the front hall. Ma stopped doing maternity calls at night and took up a regular job at the hospital. Master Ferguson got smaller and the split cane got phased out. I started noticing the big handguns the RUC wore. Basically, things got more complicated and they've stayed that way ever since.

My Mother's Daughter

Ivy Bannister

'You're late,' my mother says sharply.

I am not. I take particular care not to be late, but I feel defensive nonetheless. My mother looks me over from head to toe. Although faded by age to a watery blue, her eyes retain their power to strike me with a sudden breathlessness, and all my inadequacies, both real and imaginary, bubble to the surface.

'That dress is too young for you, Polly,' she says. 'One of your daughters should be wearing that dress.'

My three young daughters refuse to accompany me on these visits, but I don't press the issue. Perhaps I don't like them to see me through my mother's eyes.

Her handbag waits on the bed, an exquisite relic of the 1940s, brocaded and elegant. With a vigour extraordinary for her years, she flings herself into her coat.

'And how is Victor?' my mother demands, not waiting for the answer, as she bustles out of her room. I trot after her, as though I were a child again. 'When people ask after me,' she says, 'tell them the truth, Polly. Explain how you've put me into a cage and thrown away the key. I don't know how you can sleep at night, knowing what you've done to me.'

It is six months now, since my mother signed herself into the nursing home, before informing her few surviving acquaintances that I'd done the dirty on her. I overheard her on the telephone, basking in the badness of her thankless daughter. 'Sharper than a serpent's tooth,' she enthused, wielding her most thrilling tones. 'What can you expect? You give up your life for them, then they dump you into the old peoples' home.'

My mother is a very dramatic lady. Indeed, nearly a lifetime ago, she played Juliet at the Gate Theatre.

I follow her down the green and yellow corridor towards the lift. In spite of her bad hips, her bearing is regal.

The fine black cloth of her coat billows about her ankles like a coronation robe. It is impossible not to admire her. I have always admired her, and would have been glad of her admiration in return.

'I am like a caged beast in this place,' she says.

'There is nothing stopping you from moving out. They're building new flats near Seapoint.'

'Hah!' she snorts. 'Flats are for yuppies. Besides, there are not enough people about the place in a flat.' She bows her head, taking an imaginary curtain call before an imaginary audience.

The corridor smells, that tang peculiar to nursing homes of cabbage and disinfectant and urine. Sometimes at night, when I'm on my way out to a film or to a party, ready to have a good time, that smell rushes out from nowhere, burrowing up my nostrils and fogging my head. It clings to my clothes, staining the fabric of my evening with its melancholy.

The long corridor snakes around the corner, where the double windows let in a flood of light. In the recess, half-a-dozen wheelchairs are congregated, cradling the oldest and least competent inhabitants of the nursing home, a tidy row of ancient women and men, blankets tucked around them as they dribble and doze and stare.

'Just look at them,' my mother sniffs. 'Old bats! I ask you, what does a woman like me have in common with the likes of them? They are an unanswerable argument for euthanasia.'

If they hear her, in their wheelchairs, they don't react.

'Old bats!' she repeats, a shade lower, then grins, clicking her teeth.

Out the windows, you can see Bulloch Harbour and the bay. A cloud passes, its purple shadow skimming over the green sea below. I have often watched that beautiful sea from other vantage points, watched it glimmer and swirl from blue to green to grey, then back again. All of a sudden, I grab the nearest wheelchair, wheeling it around so that its aged occupant faces the water.

'Just what do you think you're doing, Polly?' my mother

demands.

'Why shouldn't they look out instead of in?'

Her lips curl into a lemony smile. 'You daredevil you. If the nurse catches you, she'll eat you.'

But I swing all the wheelchairs around, just the same. 'Hurry on,' my mother says, tapping her neat foot. 'You are too sentimental for words. No doubt you'd play Beethoven to them, if you got the chance.'

My mother brushes an empty crisp packet off the passenger seat, before she sits into the car. 'I didn't let you eat crisps,' she says, 'not when you were your daughters' age. It will give them spots.'

Cautiously, I pull out into the Ulverton Road.

'Of course, I should have drowned you when you were born,' she adds reflectively. 'That's what they do with unwanted kittens.'

I am accustomed to her saying things like this. Most of the time, I try to believe that she doesn't mean them maliciously, that it's just her habitual way of communicating.

At difficult moments you need to be pleasant, my husband Victor says. So I think pleasant thoughts about home and my work and my daughters.

'I was forty-two years of age when you were born,' my mother says, 'the same age that you are now. It was a ridiculous age for calving, the single undignified episode in my entire lifetime.'

I concentrate on the road. As I turn onto the Blackrock bypass, a few substantial drops of rain splatter onto the windscreen.

'You never fetch me out of my cage on a sunny day,' my mother says. 'Yesterday the sun shone all day. You should have come yesterday.'

She snaps open her brocaded handbag, taking out a nail file. Her fingernails are still the perfect red ovals that I remember from my childhood. I used to wonder at those perfect shapes, longing to become a woman like her.

In fact, I have not turned out badly. I work in biological

research, and my opinions about viruses and related creepy-crawlies are chronicled from time to time by the media. Victor and I get on very well together, and our rearing of our children, if not exactly seamless, has so far avoided major disaster. Three peas in a pod: that's what my mother calls my daughters, reflecting unfavourably upon how they resemble their father.

The traffic crawls around Stephen's Green. My mother is growing impatient. 'I hope that you won't park too far away. Last time, I got a blister on my instep from the distance that you made me walk.'

Since the Drury Street carpark is full, I settle for the double yellow line in front of the shoe-shop, praying without conviction for mercy from the traffic wardens. I don't blame my mother for her impatience. At the age of eighty-four, I expect that I'll be impatient too.

In Bewley's she marches back through the crowd towards the plush seats under the stained glass windows, while I queue for coffee and sticky buns. By the time that I join her, she is daubing her eyes with tissues. 'This isn't the way that it used to be,' she complains. 'There were waitresses then, and the almond buns actually tasted of almonds.'

I remember it well, my mother in her prime, whooshing past the tables in full sail, dazzling in her red cape and impossibly tall fur hat. Heads turned for her then, and the air buzzed with excited recognition. But nobody knows my mother anymore. I understand that it's not absent waitresses or inferior buns that have brought the tears to her old eyes. My heart aches, but I know better than to offer comfort. She would only brush me away.

'So,' she says brusquely, 'tell me something interesting, Polly. Impress me.'

There is no point in talking about my research, towards which she manifests a studied indifference. So I rattle on about my daughters, their enthusiasms and loathings, their flute lessons and mathematical prizes. I suspect that my mother is listening, even though her eyes sweep round and

round the tea-room. She smooths her hair with a stagey gesture. The huge diamond still glitters on her hand, only her
fingers have gone bony, and the loose ring has polished the
skin beneath with its weight. I remember that hand, taut-
skinned and plump, buttering bread, spreading jam as thick-
ly as any child could desire. I remember those eyes, laughing
and loving me. I remember loving my mother so much that
the very possibility of her going away, or dying, filled me
with the blackest terror. Perhaps she was really not as bad a
mother as she lets on to have been.

A girl passes our table in a flapping dress, unbuttoned
from hem to crotch, exposing lavender tights and heavy
black shoes. 'And she thinks she looks gorgeous,' my mother
sniffs. 'You used to do things like that to me, Polly. You
shamed me with your vulgar clothing. Not to mention those
misfits that you fell in love with. I'll never forget that
dreadful what's-his-name from Crumlin, the one whose eyes
moved in opposite directions.'

I smile brightly at my mother, pretending that I feel no
pain, but I'm glad that our coffee's drunk and it's time to go.

She is quiet for most of the journey back, melted into the
passenger seat, every muscle relaxed. It is the way she often
behaves, as if reserving her energies for her next perform-
ance. Suddenly, she pulls herself upright. 'What I resent the
most about you, Polly,' she says softly, 'is how happily you
married. Your father was such a peasant. He never had what
I wanted, not when I wanted it.'

Cautiously, I glance at her. It's a possibility I've never
considered before: that she might be envious. She glints at
me with a seabird's eye, about to devour a sprat. Then I remember a day trip, twenty years in the past, when she tried to
cajole Victor, then my fiancé, into marrying another girl. I
shiver once again at this treachery.

'When I was growing up, we had a maid named Polly,'
my mother hisses. 'She was an ignorant Welsh girl. I named
you after her.'

I can't take anymore. I pull the wheel hard, turning the

31

corner into the nursing home drive so fast that the gravel spits under my tyres. I speed recklessly through the narrow stone archway into the carpark. I jump out. The passenger door creaks open. I am counting the seconds now.

We drag through reception into the lift. My mother has begun to smile. She looks younger than her eighty-four years, and somehow radiant. I follow her into her room. 'I'm feeling quite refreshed now,' she says. 'You'd be surprised how I look forward to our little encounters.'

My chest is tight. My head is thumping. I brush my lips against her stiff cheek. Not bothering with the lift I flee down the stairs, out, out into the sea air. I barely make it to the car before the tears come, cascading down my cheeks. With shaking hands, I light the single cigarette of my week; I smoke, gasping through my tears.

Then I square my shoulders and become myself again, Polly McKenna, the capable woman created by my failed efforts to dazzle my mother, the woman that other people know and respect. And once again, I am no longer my mother's daughter. At least not for another week.

The Blind Arch

Michael Coady

I always loved it on a morning like this, the way the rising sun touches the slope over the river first of all. Then the way it floods down on the roofs and through the eight arches of the old stone bridge, except for the blind arch under the quay where the stream turns into the dark and then out below at an angle. Not that it matters at all now whether the sun is shining or the tide coming or going. Or whether wind is whining through the arches or November mist in the laneways or hard frost over the town clock or torrents of rain down Bridge Street in the small hours with not a sinner out. Still, there's something about morning sun that goes straight to the heart of things.

Here comes your man now on the bike, round the bend at the top of the hill, past the milkman who's surprised to see him out this early and down to the bridge where Oblong Ryan is already out casting a line for salmon, with Ellen gone off for the day with a busload of the Third Order of Saint Francis on a mystery tour, ending with the vigil at the moving statue outside Cappoquin. And there's the town clock bell that's sounding since Mozart was alive in the world, though you'd never know when to believe the hour that it tells.

In any case here he is again today with the pen and the big red notebook to take down all the particulars – repose of the soul of, in loving memory and all the rest of it. Repose of the soul. How easy it is once you're through and out on the other side. Alfie I said to him the first time he took me out on the river, Alfie, I said, take me back to dry land before you put the heart crossways in me. And he swung the cot in under the weir and shot her in under the blind arch of the bridge where it was pitch dark until he sank the paddle into the tide to turn her sideways and then all of a sudden we were through the tunnel and out on the stream below with

33

the light dazzling our eyes.

Seen from where the others are looking this slope that the morning touches first is a place of tears. Parting with children was worst of all, although I had none of my own. The little white box going into a hole in the ground. Enough to break the heart inside of you and leave you demented. Enough to make you want to throw yourself into the tide. And the girls and young men that coughed their way here with consumption. My own brother Martin only nineteen with the cold sweat on him and my mother beside herself holding him in her arms as he was going. Oh Jesus there's enough pain and misery in the world to earn us all heaven twice over and no questions asked.

Well there's no fear of us here, beyond all harm and on our way to some kind of salvation. Adrift in this dream while we wait for the last great call and, mother of God, that will be the day and no mistake. The big finale with the entire company brought back on the stage. In our own shapes mind you, or so we used to believe before they did away with the Latin. *Et exspecto resurrectionem mortuorum.* Because we wouldn't be our own true selves without the four bones we were born with. In the twinkling of an eye. At the last trumpet. Some music it will take to gather up all the pieces and put them together again. Professor Gebler at the organ in Waterford cathedral when I was a student. *Never fear mistakes when you play! Great music means that there is nothing to fear. Surrender yourself to the music. It tells us that the soul must never be afraid.*

They pass through here regularly, the ones that are still above ground. Taking the handy short cut from Friary Height to Abbey Square. Going for milk or rashers or the morning paper. Some that would talk the teeth out of a saw. *You remember him, he had a shop at the top of Oven Lane, that was married to Kitty Banks, she used to make lovely bread.*

Some that would argue the toss with Christ and his blessed mother. And some not sober coming back from their morning errands. Charlie Cleary talking to himself as he shuffles in the gate, tripping over kerbstones in broad daylight. Sitting down to get his bearings on top of Theobald

O'Donnell Esq and his beloved wife Hanora. Singing *Oh if I had the wings of a swallow*, as soon as he gets his wind. *I would travel far over the sea*, as he relieves his bladder behind a celtic cross carved by hand before the Boer War. Rows and arguments they carry in here as well. Whether he should go down on top of his wife or his mother. Who went where before and who comes next in order. Sacred Heart the things that bother them. And all of us easy in the one bed where there's room for all comers and one as good as the next, with flowers springing up over the lot of us though you might call them weeds if you were that particular.

So look at your man now doing the rounds of this place with poppies standing up red between the grey stones and crosses. No end of insects working away in the grass and weeds, the birds singing and all the particulars going down from stone on to paper. The sun climbing over the hill and the tide flooding up to the weir below. My own house down there too with the windows bricked up nowadays and a young sycamore growing out of the chimney.

Maybe he's learning something from the census he's taking though there's lots not written on stone. I could tell him the lovely man that his grandfather was and a good musician considering that he taught himself anything he knew. A bit of a chancer too though I never told anyone that did I? On the narrow stairs down from the organ-loft after Midnight Mass on Christmas Eve, with the two of us married already. Some drink on his breath of course and I gave him a piece of my mind. Trying to kiss me inside the church and no shame on him. What women know about men could break windows all over the town. He's down there below now with Minnie that held out twenty years after him in spite of her bad hip. And her people that thought him a fool for playing the fiddle instead of minding the shop. Not much talk out of them now with all the bad debts gone away with the tide.

I suppose if I knew him before Alfie I might have married him, with the music such a great draw between us. We had an understanding anyway with nothing ever said. He'd always wait on when I played a piece after Mass even though they'd be the last out of the church. Minnie by-the-way listening beside him that wouldn't know Bach from three blind mice. Closer than that we never got apart from that kiss on Christmas Eve.

Anyway it was all decided before that between Alfie and myself. My freshwater sailor from Passage East. *I'm a qualified marine engineer that sailed the three sister rivers since I was a boy.* Ructions raised by his people and my own as well because he was a Protestant. But we bested them all except for the fact that we had neither chick nor child and some of them thought it a judgment.

I'm a freshwater sailor washed up on the tide, he said the very first time I met him at the regatta dance when he asked me to play the piano for his party piece. A small enough man, but a voice as deep as a cave. I felt some kind of shock down to my toes when I heard him that night filling up the boathouse and silencing everyone there. *And when sergeant death in his cold arms shall take me, and lull me to sleep with his Erin go bragh.* Then letting on that he wanted lessons in reading music and voice training so that he could come calling.

Oh yes they had a mind to block us but we bested them all and had our own time and our sweetness. One night I'll never forget when we were newly married I went down by boat on the quiet with him as far as Waterford, though he could lose his job as skipper if Mr Malcolmson ever found out. A tartan rug wrapped around me sitting beside him at the wheel, with a brandy flask between us and sweet-cake. The moon shining and the tide in The Long Reach so still and perfect that you'd swear you could walk across it like Our Lord.

How innocent the river looks. Like a cat in the lap of the land. But the wildness there just under the skin. That night in December below Portnaboe, Jack Dwyer making tea in the galley when he felt her swinging out of control and up on a mud-bank. Running up to find Alfie gone over the side and beyond his reach in the dark. With myself at home in bed asleep and innocent not knowing that Malcolmson would be at my door in his stiff collar at seven in the morning. And no sign of him then or ever after though they dragged for weeks in the worst of the winter all the way down the estuary.

The rest of it was nights and days and whiskey and not caring what I did or who saw me. If only they found him I could have worked my way through it in time. If only they found him I could have grieved like many another and made up some face for the world. If only they brought some part of him home to me. The Christmas Eve I fell face down at the organ and Father Benignus told me I'd have to resign. The night of spilling rain that the guards picked me up on the bridge in my night-dress. After that the locks and corridors, the lights and pills and faces. Was it weeks or years I was there?

How easy it is in the end once you let go. Though he's not with me here I know that all is well. All is well though everything slips from our grasp. Though everything breaks and crumbles.

Here on the slope your man is fishing for names and dates that are told on stone. Maybe he'll learn it's not about things fixed on stone at all, but about a river of moments where everything filters down to the bed and nothing at all is lost. On the bridge Oblong Ryan flexes the greenheart rod in the sunshine and sends a long line curving over the pool below the weir, hoping to have a salmon laid out in the scullery when Ellen gets home tonight from her mystery tour.

Behind Glass
(*or* My Life with Bishop Berkeley)

Pat Boran

'**A** toast!' someone declared, lifting a burnt, dry slice towards the camera.

'To poverty!'

'To youth!'

'To the joys of living three to one cramped bedsit!'

Everyone had his say, her say, before the camera flashed and caught us there in our student years, two weeks before our first first-year exams, not a decent meal in days, not a bob between us, yet somehow pissed as newts (excuse the language, but it comes or came with the territory).

One, two, three, four. Count them. Seven! Seven of us. Three girls to four lads. I know what you're thinking, I bet it was your man who missed out. Why else would he be bothering to tell the story? He's obviously the one who didn't make it to Happy-Ever-After Land. And you'd be right! Look at the six happy beaming faces and then look to the left. That's me with the long face, out there against the horrendous wallpaper on my own, trying desperately to look uninterested in the carousing, the Bacchanalia, the couple-ology. That's me affecting a serious, late-teenage scowl, an intellectual furrow pasted on my brow. That's me on the tenth of June, nineteen eighty-three. I bet you don't even remember. I bet you were too busy framing the scene for posterity.

Snap! How arbitrarily eternities begin.

But don't get me wrong, I know you had other things on your mind. Your own life, for instance. And I couldn't fault you on that. I'm not here attempting to place the blame at anyone's feet or on anyone's head or in anyone's hands. I'm not attempting to pass on guilt like some physical burden. If the Good Bishop has taught me anything it's not to try to unload your grief on others. For a start, you can't depend on others. You don't even know who others are, for heaven's sake.

Who was anybody then? Who were those people I lived with and shared breathing room with? I can hardly remember them. I know what their snoring sounded like and I can still smell the clutches of dirty socks on the bedroom floor, but I know not where they came from nor where they went. I saw them as their paths crossed mine briefly, and we exchanged words.

'Are you coming out for a drink tonight?' or 'What about the party, James?'

'I don't think so,' I'd say, and then creep to the window to watch them swagger off down the road to the students' bar, whistling at every female that passed, whooping at some joke they'd heard or told already forty times before. Talking about me, too, no doubt, laughing at me behind my back. But that I didn't mind. I was never one to mind the opinion so long as I was in the thoughts of others. Much and all as I disliked them, I envied them their carefreeness, their frivolity, their abandon. Once, for instance, they tried to flag down a female professor's car right outside the door. I was transfixed there at the window by their bravery; silent, awestruck, an insect behind the glass.

You first met me, or I first met you, or whatever, in the college library. It was a couple of months before the night you mysteriously turned up at that party in our house and took this photograph before you left. I was lugging Berkeley off the topmost shelf and almost knocked myself out with it when I saw you. You wore the reddest red dress, the loudest possible colour in that most silent of places. I was so brown, so dowdy, as enclosed as the well-thumbed books, you passed without noticing me.

In fact, if there was an image that would sum up our relationship it would have to be that one: you in a blaze of your own light; me, as Shakespeare had it, darkling.

And our theme tune, the music if they ever made a film

of us, would be the hushed rustle and panicked heartbeat of a library. And maybe the swish of your dress against your thighs as you passed. Just for the pathos.

'A toast,' someone repeated, and, unbelievably, they laughed again and called for more photos to be taken, and assumed even more lurid and self-degrading poses; but you had all the evidence you wanted by then, all the proof and effects to confront me these years later with the crime of my foolishness, my shyness, my youth. You thanked us – us! – for the drinks, made your excuses, as they say, and left. I followed you to the door on the pretext of simply doing my duty as the only sober member of the party, but someone was already there before me: Grant, that plastic American with the designer teeth who wasn't even interested in you, in love only with himself and his reputation, merely up to his habitual flirting.

'Will you be all right getting home on your own?' The smarmy cretin. And saying it as loudly as he could to play to the audience inside. His own girlfriend even laughed, but I seem to recall she 'accidentally' spilled a glass over him before the night was out.

You'd wisely chosen your time to depart. Even with Grant leering beside me, I thought: if she looks back now, I'm going out there to talk to her.

But Grant had other ideas.

'Grab yourself a beer there, Plato.' He punched me on the arm.

Then the laughter again and the cheering and the music suddenly up so loud that I wanted to smash the record player (even though it was my own). And the frenzy of all of them pushing to see the photograph mysteriously developing before their eyes. (I only saw it days later when I discovered it, bent and forgotten behind a sofa cushion, and I was interested then, not in those who could be seen, but in you who couldn't.) So instead I avoided the melee. I listened to the gutted thump of party music from the lavatory or the tiny kitchen and wondered how far down the evening road

40

towards town you could still hear the sounds of my pain.

I'll tell you something about Berkeley in case you don't know, in case you haven't come across him since. I don't mean to be insulting, but lots of people quite happily and successfully get through life without knowing dot all about our friend George B.

Well, for a start, he was an Irish philosopher and bishop, who lived from 1685 to 1753, or who died when he was 68, whichever you prefer. Not a bad innings, eh, 68? Then again I suppose there's no great physical wear and tear on a philosopher. Weak eyesight, temper tantrums, withdrawal symptoms, but generally no stress or high blood pressure. And on top of that Berkeley was a bishop, so God was probably on his side a little more than usual.

Nevertheless Hegel made it to sixty-one, and Aristotle was sixty-two. Immanuel Kant and Plato himself reached the fine old age of eighty. They say that orchestra conductors live longer on average than people in any other profession. Something to do with the restorative quality of music, no doubt. But where would that leave me in my gloom and silence: condemned to die before my thirtieth birthday? I can only hope that a precedent has now been set by these enduring philosophers, and that philosophy will sustain me a modicum longer, clutching the stretcher at either end to carry me, ever more dependent for support, onward through my years.

You think *this* is a depressing picture? Wait till you hear about Berkeley!

What did Berkeley believe about objects? You'll be interested in this, being, as you are, fond of the camera and the world of images. Berkeley, if I've got him right – and he's not an easy one – Berkeley reckoned that objects (and to a photographer, that's just about everything, no?) objects exist only when they're being perceived! Get that? Only when they're being perceived. Close your eyes, or ears, nose, nerve-endings, taste-buds – and they're gone! Ka-pow! In a flash. Gone. No more.

41

I was afraid for you for months after I read that, afraid to blink when I saw you in case you disappeared, afraid that, insignificant as I was in the background of your life, when you tired of the camera and no longer saw me, even briefly, among my friends, I'd be gone forever for you, too, blank as a piece of photographic paper accidentally exposed.

That's what I was like in those days – fatalistic to the point of heroism. I followed you everywhere and worried constantly when you went away for weekends. I kept this photograph with me wherever I was, not to prove that I had been and therefore was – *that* I mostly wanted to forget – but that *you* had existed, that behind the eye of the camera was the beholder.

And surely that is no small thing, no small tribute or trivial accolade I give you now, selflessly (if someone without a self can truly be said to be able to give anything). I created and kept alive a version of you that you would never know and that I could never know myself, by definition. When people ask me how were my college years, you can imagine how difficult it is for me to talk about my studies as pursuits in and of themselves. For nothing I did was not intimately connected with you. I saw you down those summer-lit corridors, and it was as if we were at opposite ends of a telescope: you radiant, magnified, magnificent, eclipsing the sun; me, tiny, lost, a weightless mote amongst enormous tomes.

And yet, against hope, I imagined our existences were interdependent, that you could not survive without me as I could not without you. And I came to believe that we were like planets at our apogees, the most distant points of our orbits, and that we could only become closer over time. I believed that the telescope was already extended as far as it could be.

Needless to say, I was wrong.

The last time I saw you – and you'll remember this, you'll remember me from this if from nothing else I've said – the last time was when I was sitting at the entrance to the exam

42

hall for my finals. Philosophy, of course. I had my head down, not in a book – it would have been too late for that, and anyway I'd studied hard – but examining the ground, the step immediately below me. I was looking at the ants that the long dry summer months seemed to have conjured from nothing.

No one could remember ever having seen so many ants around as were around that summer. We had them in the house, in the kitchen, even in the bedroom. They scaled the bare walls to the press in a perfect line as if they were climbing an invisible rope to the promise of food. And I was drawn to them; to their power in numbers; to the notion that they were so inextricably linked, like an army, one to another, you could hardly call any one of them an individual. None could have survived without the rest. None could have believed that if he shut his eyes, *à la* Bishop Berkeley, the rest would cease to exist. He could feel their existence in his blood.

I was thinking this, or some such thing, when I looked up and there you were. Like the vision of erotic beauty saints and suicides have the night before they chose their paths. Photographing again, this time some clown in his birthday suit, stood defiantly and mockingly before the students anticipating doom, stepping in an instant from his trousers into the Drunken Yobbos Hall of Fame.

And you were photographing his moment of glory and courage. *His* moment. While all *my* moments and hours and months of perseverance and faithfulness went unseen, lost in the background still.

And that was it. I stood up then, and I approached you. And it was I who screamed, 'I never want to see you again,' and glared at you, a stranger, before I ran into the dark examination hall.

The Lost Citadel

Mary O'Donnell

Until today, the only guarantee of escape was to swim. Thea says it's an obsession. Perhaps it is. Either way, every evening at six I drive to the shore and strip to my underpants. If the tide is high, I wade out to the Gull Rock, until the waves buoy me in such a way that I am deposited quite gently on the shelf. My backside has grown accustomed to the abrasions of mussel-shell and limpet.

Then I clamber across the southernmost tip and prepare to dive. In that moment the sea drowns everything, receives my pale flesh with its own visceral embrace. Imagine the weight of thoughts that float out of every swimmer into the ocean! How easily we are absorbed by our first element, how becalmed the mind as the body dives!

What I can never fully explain to Thea, is almost inadmissible, even to myself. The sea has always helped. Until today, that is.

I know that by the time I have begun to pat myself dry and unpeel my sodden pants, she will have collected the child from the creche after work, that as I walk in the door she will in all probability be making him eat his tea, or making him wash his hands. *Making* being the operative word.

So, today, it all rushed back, as it does occasionally, a feeling that sparkles like ice or diamonds impaled in me with chill precision. Even though the whole thing happened a year ago.

The memory always coincides with conflict of some kind. And besides, we had had a bad row only yesterday. She said I exaggerated, that I overreacted.

'I – do – not – overreact!' I answered in a staccato voice.

I would rather spoil him, as she would call it, than do the opposite. Much as she wishes it, I will not collude in the strategies of adult tyranny.

'It's not tyranny!' she practically scoffed. 'Someone has to discipline the child, for God's sake, even if you can't!'

'There are other ways. There *are* other ways to ...'

'Like what?' she challenged. 'You tell me how we stop him screaming night after bloody night when he knows we're in the house, when there's absolutely *nothing* wrong with him!'

I was helpless to respond. His screams return again and again, circling my skull, jabbing at my stomach.

Today the tide was quiet, viridescent, then as I struck out, the sun spattered the bay between Giant's Crag and the Cove. I might not have ventured in, had I sensed what would occur. The air seemed warmer than on land. Not for the first time, only minutes into my swim, I detected that rank odour. It is distinctive. Smoke. The kind of smoke that wafts from food being cooked in the open, smoke and charred animal flesh.

Thea and I can talk about such things, the unusual, the singular, or the inexplicable. Naturally, she long ago concluded that it was a folk memory, though how a folk memory can strike the olfactory senses is beyond me, even if the old Norman citadel was located right there above the cliffs, even if it was big and bustling and a place for trading.

For a woman of such intuition, she can be harsh where the child is concerned. Dim, dare I say it.

I always looked forward to the prospect of bringing him out with me, of gradually teaching him about water, and about his own strength and weakness. Of course, he's only six. And when I pick up the acrid tang of smoke and flesh on the sea air I wonder, will he ever smell what I smell? And will his eyes come to rest on the cliff face as mine do, probing the crinkled erosions? Will he casually search the tawny encrustations for traces of lost settlements, places where men and boys were joyous and sure of themselves, now buried beneath the sand-martin's nests and the kittiwake ledges?

Backwards and forwards we go, Thea and I, like contestar.ts in some kind of batting game. Except that one of us doesn't always want to bat ball and the other is all too eager. Every so often she talks about women always being left to do the disciplining and then getting blamed for it.

'You're lily-livered where he's concerned. What're you afraid of?' she goads, the veins in her forehead bulging with anger.

When she comes out with that I grit my teeth. How many domestic crimes are averted through the most rigid self-control, a seizing up of the facial muscles as the weak or inadequate or irresponsible spouse stands accused by an all-too-triumphant partner?

Not for the first time I thought again today of the lies spoken in the name of childhood. That childhood is a time of inviolate growth, that there is peace and discovery and fun. Lies, lies.

This evening, I came into the kitchen wearily. My hands were still cold, unusually so, the fingers tingling with numbness. There he was, struggling with his shoes, which she claims he should by now be able to manage himself. He looked too innocent, too innocent by far, grunting and whining as he forced the left shoe onto his right foot. She could see him too. She sat quite still, feet curled beneath her on the sofa, her nose, as usual, in a book.

I bent to help him. She looked up and sighed.

'Can't you let him be?' she said, not unkindly. 'He has to learn for himself.'

'But we have to show him, Thea.'

'If I've shown him once I've shown him forty times. Can't you see – it's all for *attention*!'

Once more, beaten into a cul-de-sac. He stopped pulling at the shoe, tugged it off again and ran towards me.

What torments me most is the quality of his forgiveness, which seems absolute, and not marred by fear. And yet I wonder at his notes, the scrawled messages delivered to both our pillows in new, shaky writing.

'To Daddy and Mammy, you are good to me.'

Or 'Thank you Daddy and Mammy. I love you. I will be good.'

I quake at the thoughts of him. I still hear his scream. I still see the little legs kicking out in an attempt at childish defiance which he could not easily sustain.

And again, again, I ask myself why I did it, why I listened to her?

For a short while today, the sea soothed me. This time I stripped completely standing by the jeep, fired my clothes into the torn passenger seat. Pieces of his lego-set lay on the floor. Complete nakedness felt good. There was nobody around, except for a mooning couple some few hundred yards up towards the sand-bar, too absorbed in one another to notice a pale, greying man.

I was cleansed again, swam eight hundred yards breaststroke, turned and swam eight hundred more front crawl, turned again and backstroked, my eyes open and my head singing with the sounds of ocean and gull, and the smell of the Norman fires which I now took for granted rushing to my nostrils, and then – at first I wasn't certain – voices. Mens' voices, powerful laughter, which crushed over my body and faded too suddenly, as if washed through with something more sinister.

Then I heard it, as clearly as if Thea and I were in the bedroom, or arguing in front of the child, or at our own hearth with the logs hissing and the coal crackling. Well out of my depth, I stopped swimming and floated, my ears throbbing.

Not even the sea could save me. The current beneath became a shaft of ice, fixing me in a state of solid fear. But it was more than the current, and I continued to float in an attempt to recover my equilibrium, told myself that it would be all right, that things would sort themselves out in time, that time was a healer. Yet when the ancient voices faded, all I could hear was one child's voice, the screams and the fear of one child as I tried to please her, doing my best to see things her way. It was the middle of the night. He'd been calling for hours, whinging and sobbing. Finally, it was my turn, and I bore her rage like a ball of steel, grabbing him from beneath the bed-clothes. He roared as I shook him. Then I struck and could not stop. I flailed at his legs and arms with my man's strength, as if to finally quieten him, or show him that this was the way and once and for all, he would behave for her.

47

'No Daddy! No Daddy! Oh please, no Daddy, I'll be good, I will Daddy, oh Daddy!' he wailed and gulped, slipping once more from my grasp and running to the bathroom, where I missed him again and he jumped into the bath, screaming, the tears bursting from him, crouching finally, hands over his head as my blows rained down and his forehead struck the faucet.

Thea stopped me, her face white and wet.

'Not that much, not that much!' she called, catching my arm ...

I think I almost drowned this afternoon. Perhaps I wanted to. Or else it was my own weeping, inaudible amidst all that water and salt, a great weight crushing my lungs as I lost my breath and slipped under for those few moments.

I love the smell of him. His skin. His soft hair. His breath, which is always sweet.

There is nothing he cannot – could not – do, given the right chance. There is nothing we could not accomplish, a father and a son. I would die for him.

Billy in the Summer of 1962

Aodhan Madden

On a bright June day in 1962, my brother Billy decided to become a priest. I can remember the exact moment. We were having a family picnic on the beach at the Hoare Rock in Skerries. There had been a light rain shower and as the cloud moved off to the east, we caught a glimpse of the Mourne Mountains. 'That's what St Patrick saw from Wales,' said Billy with great seriousness. He took off his spectacles and wiped them with his handkerchief. Then he peered out to sea again. The Mournes melted ghostly into a skein of cloud.

Billy seemed to be the only one dressed on the beach that day. He was sixteen and already seemed old to us. I remember Ma looking at him strangely. 'Would you like a sandwich?' she asked him, but he shook his head impatiently. I knew God had whispered something in his ear because he was trembling.

'I'm going to be a priest,' he said gravely. Ma said nothing for a moment. Then she shrugged her shoulders as if a cold wind had come up from the sea. 'Well I hope that won't put you off your grub,' she said with a hint of mockery. We all laughed, relieved that the solemn moment had passed, and dived into the sandwiches.

A look was exchanged between Billy and Ma. It meant nothing to me then. But years later when memory had sharpened the focus of that family picture, I saw that look again. It was the briefest betrayal of some vague fear.

Skerries, that June, seemed bathed in a certain light. I first noticed it one day when we were passing Red Island. Two elderly English ladies were gazing out to sea. They were windswept and they giggled like schoolgirls. Their faces were pinker than the hydrangeas on their gaudy skirts, but all about them was this intense white light as if I saw them in a dream. I thought of St Patrick and his Pascal fire.

The light spread from the harbour, over the south beach

and out as far as Loughshinney. I could see the boys and girls jiving to Elvis Presley songs outside the amusement arcades below. Occasionally, some of them stopped dancing and gazed seawards. I saw Billy frown. He said there were great troubles brewing up in the world outside.

One evening we were sitting on the beach outside our house. The tide was in. As the beach at the Hoare Rock sloped steeply into the sea, the effect on this starlit night was like sitting on the edge of the universe. Somebody was singing. I think it was Alfie Ryan who lived in a tent in the Mill Field. My parents and aunts Kate and Eileen had come back from Joe May's pub and they were talking heatedly about Khrushchev.

Suddenly my aunts joined in the singing. I sensed an uncomfortable note of defiance as they warbled 'Beautiful Isle of Somewhere' to the night. Ma held my father's hand. She seemed worried about something. I thought the music was making her sad.

Then all of a sudden someone shouted 'where's the baby?' Ma screamed. Sile, who was five and no longer an infant, was presumed to be safe asleep in bed, but pandemonium broke out that night on the beach when it was discovered that she was missing. We dispersed in all directions in the dark, like Napoleon's army in the fogs of Russia. But then Billy took charge. He jumped up onto the grass bank. 'Right,' he barked with sudden authority, 'everyone split up. Ma, you go back and search the house. The rest of us will search the beach and the road.'

Ma calmed down a little when she realised that a cool head was dealing with the crisis. She said 'If anyone can find her, Billy will', and that seemed to settle it for her. Billy went off towards the rocks. I remember him saying gently to Pop, 'No, I'll look down on the beach. You try the houses.'

The huge relief when Sile was found safe and well in a neighbour's house was such that the party began once more in earnest. Neighbours, even strangers came out to join our celebration. Bottles of stout were passed around and Alfie accompanied my aunts on his guitar as they sang a very emotional version of 'Moon River' which was all the rage that summer.

Billy was the hero of that night. He tugged at his tie and beamed with embarrassed delight when Alfie raised his bottle of stout to a toast. 'To Billy,' we all shouted. 'He's going to be a priest,' Ma whispered to one of the aunts. We stayed singing on the beach until a red light crept up behind the harbour and a chorus of gulls announced the dawn.

Towards the end of that June I woke early one morning to hear someone calling out down on the strand. It seemed like a dream cry, mournful and remote. At first I thought it was the seagulls, but then I noticed Billy's voice. I looked out the bedroom window and saw him standing down at the sea's edge calling to someone in the water. He was very distressed. For a long time I couldn't see anybody in the water.

I began to think that he was talking to Saint Patrick who once lived in Skerries and whose presence Billy swore he often felt. Then a figure walked from behind the big rock and waded towards Billy. My heart jumped. It was Alfie Ryan. He was fully dressed. He seemed to be crying. He was clutching a bottle in his hand. Billy helped him out of the water and put him sitting on the beach.

Then I saw Ma come rushing out below with a mug of tea which she kept stirring. Something very exciting had obviously happened. I wanted to run down and see. There was something intensely private about that scene on the beach. Alfie was rocking to and fro in great distress, and Billy was behind him, hugging his shoulders. Ma held the mug to Alfie's mouth and she seemed to be coaxing him to drink. I felt a hand on my arm. It was Pop. 'Come on away,' he said gently, and he led me back to bed.

Afterwards when I mentioned Alfie, Ma just whispered: 'The poor man's gone away.' She shook her head as if forbidding any further conversation on the matter. She looked to Billy for support. I felt that I had no right to pursue this any more; children have their own keen sense of boundaries and what happened on the beach belonged to a different order of knowledge and experience than I was privy to. Yet I wondered what was so terrible about what happened to

Alfie that I could not be told.

Billy became a man that summer. He knew what he wanted to be and suddenly he was taken seriously. His opinions were avidly sought and cherished by Ma and the aunts. Everything he did and said, even the careful way he dressed, all suggested deliberate movement towards the priesthood. He never took his shoes off on the beach. In some strange way he was expected not to rough and tumble like the rest of us.

I can still see him waving the thurible at evening Benediction in the parish church in Strand Street. He did so with such professional ease that it became impossible to think of him as anything other than a priest. I can see the faces of the old women in the front pews. They gazed at Billy as if touched by grace. The idea of Billy getting married and having children, or working in an office or a building site, began to seem ludicrous. Ma started to treat him as special, someone apart.

I heard her saying to Pop a few nights after Alfie's disappearance: 'The aunts said they'll help out with the college.' Then she said: 'Does it really have to be England?' They were in bed. I heard the pride in her voice. I heard something else, something like fear. It was the first time I felt Billy would go away.

When she repeated the question 'Why does it have to be England?' I knew she was crying. God had whispered to her that he wanted Billy and she was powerless to resist. I heard the sea whispering in her room that night. I heard Pop's muffled words of comfort. I knew that once Billy went away, part of him would never come back.

Next morning, Kate and Eileen left early to catch the train to Dublin. Billy carried their luggage to the station. Kate was giddy. 'We have a gentleman at last,' she called back to Ma, and Eileen glowered at her in disapproval. Ma cried after they had gone. I think she was sensing other departures to come.

It was the last day of our holiday and I was feeling sad. Suddenly everything seemed uncertain. I walked down the beach and over to Red Island to have a last look around the

Skerries I was afraid I might never see again. The English visitors strolled trance-like around the gardens and dance music burst from the great ballroom. It was a windy, cloudless day, and that pristine light revealed that South Beach as I never saw it before.

It exposed the peeling red paint on the gaudy frontages of the amusement arcades, the shabby lettering on the fish 'n' chip stalls, the blue purity of the sea. It revealed the laughing, gawky faces of boys in drainpipe trousers and winklepicker shoes leering at posters of Mitzy Gaynor outside the Pavilion cinema. It revealed, as the glow in an old snapshot might reveal, the heightened optimism of an age.

I sat on the beach across the road from the cinema. 'South Pacific' was showing and two girls at the box office sang exultantly: 'Bali-Bough come to me on the wind of the sea' to the air of the hit song from the film, and the gaggle of boys in winklepickers booed and cheered and whistled as they streamed down the strand.

Something was in the air. It made Ma uneasy and it filled Billy with certainty. It made the English visitors gloomy as they walked in circles around Red Island. It stirred a kind of madness in the teenagers jiving to the rhythms of the age. It made me apprehensive. I had overheard my aunts whispering about Khrushchev and the end of the world. I wondered what Alfie saw out beyond the Hoare Rock. Why did Billy really want to become a priest? Did he too sense menace creeping across the world?

He sat down beside me. I don't know how he found me. All through my childhood he turned up in my most private places.

'It's time to go home,' he said. I wanted to hold him. I wanted to protect him from that God who was going to take him away from us.

He must have sensed my confusion because he took my hand and squeezed it and held it to his forehead for a moment. 'Why does it have to be in England?' I heard myself ask.

He didn't answer. I felt him trembling. I needed to scream then, like a child who had sensed some irreplaceable loss.

He tugged my hand. 'C'mon,' he said with sudden briskness, 'enough of your day-dreaming.'

We both walked back to the car in silence.

Tompkins Square Park

Margaret Dolan

'Okay lady,' the men said when I explained from behind the closed apartment door that I couldn't let them in, because I was only a guest there.

When they came back banging on the door, shouting 'Open up lady', fear buzzed in my head like a trapped bluebottle churning up the chef, the ballet dancer and the soup. Taking my breath away.

I awoke shivering on the floor. The men gone. I took my coat and left.

Lucky ... lucky ... lucky ...

I say it like a mantra. As I rock back and forth. Back and forth. In my big navy coat. On the park bench. Me and the Indian. He doesn't rock. He doesn't do anything. Just sits. His Big-Chief head dress is stubby and broken. His stoic face bruised purple on one side. When not battered he has the palest face. Always in the park or on the edge. Always alone. Always immaculate in his Indian gear. Until today that is.

Not his day either.

Or the grey bearded man in the silky green dress, clinging to his legs above heavy boots. A matching green silk ribbon ties back his seaweedy hair. He roots in the bins, getting nothing.

Did the Indian eat the soup?

Did the old man in the green dress eat it?

The soup is always on my mind. The soup, the chef and the ballet dancer. The chef lived on the next block with the ballet dancer. I used pass their apartment every day. He made soup for the down-and-outs in the park. Good soup they said. Last time he made it, he used the ballet dancer's head. His friend testified. Saw the head in the pot. I nightmare about him and the Hispanic.

The Hispanic waiting for me. Waiting to get me. Like the American on the plane said he would.

'Some day,' he said. 'You'll be standing on the corner and this Hispanic will come along and slice your head off. No reason. Just 'cause you're there.' Then he smiled his good clean all American smile and said, 'Have a nice day'.

I told Mick and Una and they fell about laughing. Told all their friends. But I know he's out there, waiting ... I always have my key out, ready ... nearly always tear the skin off my knuckles trying to get it in the lock, fast. Always fumble.

I've seen him on the corner. Waiting. I showed Mick. He said he was a fellow from Mayo waiting for a lift. Mick's always trying to console me.

What'll he say about today?

Those men trying to break into the apartment. Beating down the door till I couldn't breathe. He'll make an excuse for them, just like Una. And they'll look at each other. And Una will have her, 'it's her or me', look.

I came for a few weeks, till I got my bearings, armed with tea and chocs and crisps. And stayed and stayed. The tea and chocs and crisps are long gone. I cling like film to Mick and Una is pissed off. Poor Mick is torn.

Can't throw out his poor little cousin, now can he?

Una hates me. I hate me. A cringing eejit. At first I was a joke. Now a burden. An intolerable burden. I cause rows. I hear them. Una saying things like, paranoid and unsuitable and not cut-out and asking for it.

'Asking for what?' he jumps in.

'To be mugged, raped, murdered or all three.'

He says he never thought he'd ever hear a fully fledged feminist like her saying such a thing.

Una explodes with 'she's so terrified, she's a pushover, she freezes if anyone looks at her.'

He says coldly, 'so she's vulnerable and needs to be taken care of and you want me to throw her to the wolves?'

And she says in her last-straw-voice, 'SEND HER HOME'.

Home, I want to go home more than anything else, but what can I do?

'A Donnelly visa,' they said. 'You lucky, lucky thing.' I hugged myself with the excitement of it all. Da kept singing 'New York, New York', when he wasn't humming 'Manhattan'. 'Say hello to Delancey Street for me,' he said. And I did.

When the train pulled in at Delancey, Una shouted, 'Hold your nose and run for it'. I ran past the homeless, the junkies, the beggars with their white plastic cups meekly uttering 'change'. The pong of urine and sweat followed me into derelict Delancey.

I never mentioned Delancey when I wrote home. Instead I eulogised about Una's super job with the fab freebies. How she brought me to see Steffi Graf in Madison Square Gardens, best seats too, and the black-tie-invitation-only painting exhibitions,where the glitterati rolled up in their chauffeur-driven limousines. NEVER a mench of the homeless, rolled up in sleeping bags in adjacent doorways.

So now I'm trapped in my big navy coat. In Tompkins Square Park. In my invented landscape.

Una comes in her power suit with her massive shoulder pads. She stands before me in her 'no-nonsense' stance. Stabbing the lean earth with her stiletto heel.

'So here you are Siobhán, you do surprise me, here of all places, who'd have believed it? Won't Mick be amazed?'

I rock faster.

'Stop that stupid rocking and listen to me, listen to me, you stupid cow, the men trying to get into the apartment were from the cable company ... the TELEPHONE COMPANY.'

I titter. She loses her cool. Her mouth opens and words pour out spilling all over the place like coins from a slot machine jackpot. All the things she wanted to call me and couldn't while Mick was around. The titters multiply into hysterical laughter and I rock so hard I'm almost in a spin. She backs away slowly. I slow down to a steady rock. I'm no longer laughing.

She's right about the park. It is ludicrous. On our doorstep, and I've never been in it before now. Even when Mick tried to inveigle me in to play basketball I wouldn't budge. I observed it daily from the safety of the apartment. Sat on a high stool with my coffee and bagels and watched the children flying high on swings, the joggers, the basketball players, the Ukrainians playing chess. The sanitised view. I knew if I moved my eyes slightly to the left I'd see THEM. The crackheads, drunks, down-and-outs, lolling on benches or in sinister groups. And maybe even the Hispanic waiting for me.

Now, the park is my refuge. I have to laugh and laugh.

Mick gathers me up and carries me back to the apartment. He holds my hands. I watch them shake as if they belong to someone else.

'You've got to write to your mother,' he says. 'Tell her how you feel, how unhappy you are, that you want to go home.'

A hairline crack in his voice. His hands tighten. His beard is sprouting little gold needles. A sliver of tomato is caught in his tooth.

Una says 'I'll get pen and paper.' Her face pleating in satisfaction.

'Auntie Kate'll understand.' Mick says.

I laugh to myself at the thought of my mother understanding. Especially after all the boasting she did to mothers of illegals.

'Of course,' she crowed. 'Our Siobhán has a green card, can do what she likes, go where she wants. Get a well paid job.'

Just stopping short of saying 'not like your lot'.

I can see them accosting her on my return.

'See your Siobhán's home.'

'Holiday,' she'd brazen.

'So soon?'

'Can come and go as she pleases.'

'Looks peaky.'

'You know these high flying executives.' She'd laugh her

58

woman-of-the-world laugh.

'When is she going back?' they'd slip in. Slyly.

'Soon, very soon,' she'd snap. 'And she's taking Seán back with her.'

'Seán?' I say, on a wave of tears.

'Ah yes, Seán,' Mick says. 'Can't be helped.'

'I'm his saviour.'

'I wouldn't go as far as that.' He smiles sadly.

'His ticket to America.'

'I know but you can't sacrifice yourself ... no one would expect ...'

'Mam.'

My tears splash on our hands. Micks's adam's apple bobs up and down. His eyes mist. He retreats into our childhood, drawing me into the garden where the Cordylions grew ... the strawberries holed by worms ... the pet jackdaw ... superman's medicine exploding, skin hanging in bubbles ... I peer into the spaces in his conversation. He shifts uncomfortably in my silence.

'Pen and paper,' Una says.

'Just a note,' Mick says, steering me towards the table. 'Tell her about today ... the park.'

I nod and sit.

'A few words'll do,' Mick encourages.

Una prattles on saying things like 'Tell them I was asking for them'. Mick keeps giving her 'shut-up' looks. But she's so relieved at my pending exit she can't. Mick says 'Cut it Una'. And she does.

I see their faces, Mam's, Dad's and Seán's. Mam's looms large. I start writing.

Dear Mam, Dad, Seán,

Eat your hearts out, you poor suckers, stuck in murky, misty, rheumy Irish November. Here in the Big Apple the air is crunchy crisp. A bright, glittery, glossy sort of day. In the park opposite, pure yellow leaves flutter to the ground making a sun carpet.

Da, you'll never believe this. Charlie Parker, Charlie 'Bird' Parker lived on the far side of the park, just across the street. When you come over you'll see the plaque.

The bad news. I think Mick and Una are about to split up. They fight all the time.

Love Siobhán.

P.S. We're out of tea bags.

The Dancing Chicken of Chinatown

Ivy Bannister

There is a case full of chicken embryos in jars of formaldehyde, somewhere in Dublin's Natural History Museum. I remember them from years ago, the time that my mother brought me to the museum. It was a couple of weeks after my Dad had beetled off to England without a return ticket in his back pocket, and I was still in short pants. The outing was intended to distract me – and maybe my mother – from fretting about my departed Dad. It wasn't meant to awaken my conscience, but as it happened, those pickled chicks are the only thing about that museum that stayed in my head.

The jars were arranged in a tidy row, and I can picture the victims quite clearly, from the tiniest reddish blob, the size of a pin-head, to the translucent feathery birdshape, arrested forever on the brink of birth. To think of it! Generations of Irish kids, noses pressed against the glass, inspecting that row of tiny corpses. I never wanted any child of mine to endure such official ghoulishness.

Not that I'll ever have a kid now. But I've been thinking about those chicks of late, even though I'm living a world away, right in the guts of New York City. There's a lively arcade on Mott Street in nearby Chinatown, a place jumping with video games, one-armed bandits and pinball machines. However, the star attraction is no glitzy machine. No. It's a wee simple cage that looks empty at first glance, only there's a velvet banner above it that reads 'The Dancing Chicken of Chinatown'. Feed 75 cents into the slot, a partition clatters up, and the bird herself appears, a little brown hen, stretching her wings. With a blast of rock music, the floor of the cage begins to spin and the hen bops and flaps and jumps like a feathery disco queen. This dancing bird is a hit with Chinese and tourists alike, and shrieks of laughter melt in

61

with the rock music, the racket of the machines and the roaring traffic outside.

Marlene. Even her name is beautiful. Silver and mysterious, a name too exotic for Ireland.

A bit of dirty cardboard has been tied onto the cage like an afterthought. Chinese characters are scrawled in black ink, with what I take to be the English translation underneath: 'This bird is happy in her work'. Well, who am I to say that she isn't. She has an appreciative audience, at least. Her feathers are sleek. Her eyes have a bright glitter to them, which I would describe as defiant, if I knew anything about chickens, which I don't. Besides, isn't the little hen better off dancing on cue, then she would be roasting in an oven, or pickled on a shelf in a museum?

Not so very long ago, defying cleaver or even imprisonment, I would have forced open the door of that bird's cage, to watch her flutter free: out from the noisy arcade and up into the night sky. But I've changed. Now I can see that life is neither black nor white, but endless shades of grey, all melting into one another, just like this incredible city. If I set that hen free, there might be nothing for her but roosting alone in a scraggy plane tree, until she starves to death. Besides, so long as she dances in her cage, that birdie is a gold mine. These are the figures as I've calculated them: 75 cents a dance, a hundred times a day, makes 75 bucks, 500 a week or 25 grand a year. And that's a wage that most of the lads back home wouldn't turn up their noses at.

Marlene. I can see her now, climbing the hill in Killiney, her full white skirt rising in the breeze. Marlene. I can hear her calling me, 'Billy boy!' As I lie on my back, I can see the leafy branches lacing over our heads like the vaulting of a cathedral.

I walk for miles in New York City, uptown and back each day, more than I ever walked in Dublin. I walk until my feet feel like lead weights, but I keep my eyes open wide and let the whole scene seep into my bones. Believe me, this crazy metropolis makes Dublin look clean and wholesome. Garbage cans overflow on every corner, and men and women root for sustenance among the pickings. There are so many people here, an endless sea of faces flashing past, faces that I'll never see again. It embraces me, this bustling anonymity. I am only in my twenties, and already I've ruined my life.

I've written to Marlene, dozens of letters, amusing letters. I've told her about the dancing chicken, but not about the sick feeling that watching her gives me, and not the fact that the cage floor is wired, and that it's electrical jolts that make her dance. Instead I've joked about setting up a similar business in Ireland. 'I know that there's no Chinatown in Dublin,' I've written, 'but I'm going to start one up. I'll plaster my eyelids down with tape and gabble like Fu Manchu. It'll make us rich, and our kids will live like gods.'

Keep it light, I tell myself, as I scribble. Make it sound like a dream, like paradise. Make her want to be with you, like that day that we went out in the boat from Dun Laoghaire pier. We sat in the back, kissing, as the boat chugged from Dalkey Island, and the wind blew Marlene's hair against my cheek. I wrapped my arm around her shoulders, curling my fingers under her breast. She sucked on my lip, whispering that she'd gone damp between her thighs.

I write to Marlene, page after page, from the dark squalid room where I sleep. As I write, I can hear the roaches scratching inside the walls. I don't tell Marlene the truth. I don't tell her lies either, but I embroider, I invent. I pretend that it's not too late to rebuild bridges. If only she'd answer just one of my letters, I'd catch the next plane home.

What happened between us was my fault. I went over the top. I lashed out at her, as if she were the enemy. My own rage shocked me. I still don't understand it, not even now. How can you suddenly hate someone so much, when the truth is that you love them? Why couldn't I listen, wait, hold on to what I had?

The sidewalks are cracked in this place. As I walk, the rubbish swills around my ankles. Night and day, sirens scream: fire engines, police cars, ambulances. Once, at the corner of 23rd and Lexington, I saw a body stretched out along the curb. It was covered in a white sheet, with the blood soaking through like red wine. A beefy New York cop stood guard, champing on gum, his revolver bulging on his hip. But nobody else was paying much attention. It's not like Dublin, where crowds gather at the hint of disaster to speculate in hushed tones. The taste buds for disaster have grown jaded here.

From the time I first laid eyes on Marlene, I pictured her with a baby. Two babies, if you want to know the truth. Twins to start out, and then some. No way was I going to be the louser that my Da was. I was going to rush home every night to my wife and kids, to look after them and love them, happily every after. Talk about romantic. That's the kind I was, really wet behind the ears. It was inevitable that, sooner or later, reality would creep in. And when it happened, I blew it. It never occurred to me what it must have cost her to do what she did.

As I walk, I can see her in my head. I'm lying in her bed, the duvet clean against my body. She has slipped out from my arms to dress. The sun lights her back with a pearly glow. Near the window, the table is laid for breakfast, the crusty loaf waiting on the bread board.

In the place where I sleep now, the light struggles through windows encrusted with grease and soot. I share with a transient crowd. A long apartment of airless rooms off a stinking corridor. My fellow tenants are illegals like myself: a Romanian, an Estonian Jew, but mostly Hispanics, coming and going, always looking over their shoulders for fear of deportation. They keep on the move, out to Jersey to pick fruit, down to Florida, to Detroit, Chicago and points further west. Nobody stays long. Nobody, that is, except me. At nine months, I have become the senior occupant. Unlike the others, my interest in my own fate has faded.

The letterbox is in the hallway below. The flap springs open when you tap the lock sharply. I often wonder if a letter from Marlene has been stolen. It's a fantasy that engages my imagination, but I don't really believe in it. Nobody would bother to nick a personal letter, not even in New York. Besides, I get regular post from my mother. She writes out the football results, and snippets of political scandal. But I sift through her words in vain for reference to Marlene. Occasionally, by return, I send my mother a twenty dollar bill wrapped in a sheet of newspaper.

Miles uptown is the apartment block where I work as a doorman. It's a massive building with a marble portico, high ceilings, thick carpet everywhere. Each apartment has an entire floor to itself. I got the position, no questions asked, because my skin is the right colour, and my English is fluent. My job is to keep the undesirables out. You'd think they'd pay me in gold nuggets, but the fact is that the dancing chicken makes out better than I do. The rich don't get rich by being sentimental. In Dublin I worked with computers, but I can't fool with that here, not with only a phoney social security number, I can't.

'It's a free country.' That's what they say all the time here. That, and 'Have a nice day'.

I often think of the sea, and what it looked like, those last minutes that I spent with Marlene. We were strolling on Sandymount Strand, well out on the flats, the wet sand cool under our feet. She nuzzled her warm lips against my hand. I asked her how she'd got on, down in the country, where she'd been to see her folks. She stared out at the water, glittering in the distance, brilliant as diamonds. I looked with her; it was so pretty. It was then that she told me that she hadn't gone down to the country after all. 'I went across the water,' she said. 'To London.' I looked at her strange, cold eyes, but I still didn't understand. I was that innocent.

So she stood there, tapping herself on the belly, her head half-cocked sideways, a nervous twist to her lips. Tapping herself on the belly, until the penny finally dropped. 'I didn't want to spoil it all, Billy boy,' she said. 'We're too young. We needed to grow up ourselves first.'

I looked at her beautiful mouth, and I hit her. A great belt on the face. I can still hear the sound of flesh meeting flesh, the crushing of cartilage. I can see the blood streaming from her nose, the hurt look in her eyes. But I turned my back on her, and ran away. Later, when I tried to call her, again and again, she wouldn't speak to me.

New York is an old people's city. It's not like Dublin, with young mothers everywhere pushing buggies. There are more geriatrics than babies on the streets of New York, out with their nurses and minders, in wheelchairs and walkers, their shaky old hands covered in loose skin.

Sometimes when I'm walking, I just stop, dead in the centre of the sidewalk. I close my eyes and stick out my elbows. I imagine my feet on a turntable with jolts of electricity sparking up through my soles. I hear the beat of rock music, thudding out over the sirens and grunting buses. I cackle, flap my arms and dance, and around me, the crowd parts, passing me by with a wide berth.

The Suit

Pat Boran

It's a strange feeling, being back. Much to my surprise, I recognise almost nothing of the place. The shopfronts I had expected to be familiar are strange, and I realise that, had I stepped down from the bus in any other midland village, I might never have discovered my mistake. Were it not for the villagers. Da, you were right about them.

The morning was warm, stilly, and, as I looked around for signs of life, a place to get a coffee or a pack of cigarettes, I noticed I was being observed from a half dozen open doorways by a half dozen villagers who'd presumably once been my neighbours. They watched closely my every move. Of course, I didn't recognise them. In my case, I saw only caricatures from the stories you used to tell about life in a world I no longer recall. Every time I try to remember this place, or the friends I must have had here, I'm left with something unreal, Da, something you invented in stories.

As far as the villagers themselves were concerned, they saw only this garish suit I stood in, this canary yellow suit flapping lightly in the breeze that stole through their silenced village square over which they kept watch from the shadowed doorways of their houses and half-stocked shops. Their world bare and open before this stranger, and they staring at his canary yellow suit. And though, as I say, I didn't recognise even one of them, and had no idea what to expect, every one of them must have known, and expected, me.

Unable to endure the curiosity of the publican, and the unspoken scorn of the men who, dressed in black, sat along his bar, I took a stroll to find what might once have been our house, but of course found nothing. It's probably in ruins now, used as a pig-pen, or the walls have been taken down and the stones used to pave a milking parlour in some nearby farm. The village children I met on my walk were more open than their parents, if hardly less hostile. They pointed at me, or rather at the suit, and jeered.

I've only ever worn it once before. Do you remember, Da? And in all the intervening years, you raising me without the benefit of a wife and mother, I've never once, until today, given in to the desire to put it on again. Wearing it that first time was an honour which, at twelve, I didn't – I couldn't – appreciate. It's importance as a symbol was way beyond me then. In fact it's taken me all these years to find an occasion that warrants putting it on again.

Arriving back here today, and standing in these heavily-starched folds, I remembered the first time – a nearby town, the church packed and humid, the rows of us before the altar, the bishop coming to a halt in front of me and finding, instead of reverence, something close to pride – pride that I had, at last, joined the ranks of adulthood, the ranks of those whose knobbly knees would for ever more be covered except in special circumstances; pride that no one would laugh this time as they did every time before at our football games and trips to the seaside. It can't have been easy to have been a skinny child in such a brutal place as this. Maybe that's why I forget almost everything about it.

I felt like a stranger getting off the bus, Da. It was weird. Forget the village, I felt like a stranger to your suit. Your showband suit, your *how's-it-goin'-doll?-is-you-mother-out?* suit, your *don't-tell-me-we're-playing-in-this-dive-for-ten-bob and-a-pint-of-lemonade!* suit. You swore it was fashionable once – Don't make me laugh! This suit's for people who already feel alien. It gives them a reason for all their unreasonable feelings, if you know what I mean. Ah, I don't know what I mean. All I know is in my Confirmation photographs, photographs I felt so proud of at the time, I now see only the horror of it all – a skinny kid lost in yellow folds, his bleary-eyed father with the bulge of a half-bottle on his hip.

'It's the poor mother I feel sorry for.'

'A saint and an angel.'

In the same canary yellow as all those years ago, I stood again today among your people. And they in turn dressed in black as they'd done before. Again they looked at me in shock or in embarrassment – I who am one hundred per cent the image of you at my age, before drink pulled you down, half-drowned you, before it smashed your guitar over a bouncer's head and left you with a bottle opener and a shaky hand.

'Built in tremelo, Marty!' But that joke wore thin.

Am I getting carried away? You see, I remember sometimes. The bouncer never recovered, but neither did you. You couldn't stop feeling guilty. And this place – village, town, call it what you like – it's never forgotten. Going home is an experiment in memory.

'Where's the gig, head? How's it going, luv? Is you mother out?'

The litany of dance-hall cracks lives on in this suit. As soon as I put it on this morning, I could hear your voice, Da. I could hear it desperate and funny, conspiratorial and drunk, melodic and melancholic. But that's it. I couldn't hear how it must have sounded saying mother's name.

In the graveyard I heard them whisper that the cut of me was a disgrace. They said I hadn't the decency to dress for the occasion, that I'd turned out just like my father, if not worse. After all, they said, I had no excuse, nothing to hide behind like you had. I could still save myself. And maybe I can.

But even above the accusations, I could hear your voice, croaking and groaning, and your useless fingers picking at guitar strings. You know, sometimes I think it would have been better if you hadn't missed it at all – the life, the road, the freedoms, the few lights there were.

You in a string vest trying to play something you bought in a pawn shop from horse winnings, six years of nervous exhaustion down the line, is not my favourite picture of you. With this pathetic memory in my head, I looked around at the neighbours who must have wondered why I bothered to attend at all. It was a puzzle to them that I hadn't stayed away and left them to commemorate your passing in a dignified manner, a manner that befitted the demise of a way-

ward son. You see, Da, my very presence caused them un-
ease. For them it was like standing beside the person they
were burying.

After the service, and with the mourners gone, I hung on
a while. I stared at the blank spot over your grave and
wondered what a stone there might say that would distinguish you from all the other half-remembered souls. The
year of your birth? You know, I've never known for certain
and, of course, could never have asked.

What else? 'Deeply regretted by', replaced with 'Old
Shep he has gone where the good doggies go'? I can't
imagine these people erecting a headstone with a guitar or a
line from an Elvis song cut into it. And I know they'd never
approve of a depiction of a bottle of whiskey, however much
you might appreciate it.

I spoke to a traveller on the way back to the village who
claimed he'd seen you perform a couple of times the best
part of twenty years ago. It's a small world; I'm sure it is
possible. He couldn't remember if you were wearing the
suit, but he had advice for me.

'Your father, now,' he said, 'your father wants you to
sing and play the music.'

'Does he?' He obviously didn't know why I was here.
'But I'm really not a musician.'

'You've growed into the suit, so you be all right.'

Maybe. I'm more inclined to think I'm finally growing
out of it. All day it's felt more and more strange. I told him
so, and we drank a toast to an independent existence for the
suit, to the suit on its own. He said he'd be very interested in
it if I wanted to let it go. Don't worry, Da, I said I'd *think*
about it.

It's after dark now, the pubs are closed, and I'm staying in a
B & B in the village you're from. Excuse me, but I feel I have
to say these things aloud to understand them. This is the
village where I grew up and couldn't have waited to leave if
we'd stayed long enough. But we never did – stay long
enough for me to want to leave. Or to remember much.

I'm still wearing your canary yellow showband suit, by the way, even as I think of this. In the pockets I find a combination of your and my things: buttons, plectrums, scraps of paper collected over the years. Do you want to know what's here? Well, for instance, here's this morning's bus ticket down from Dublin, stamped with today's date. Here's a receipt from an off-licence on the North Circular Road, £28.80, undated – it could belong to either one of us. Here's a St Christopher's medal which, I'm sure, belongs to someone else entirely, ha ha ha. Here are a few broken matchsticks that won't light. One prize toe-nail clipping. Here are some very old cigarette burns in the lining. Here's the fluff and grease and wear and tear of a thousand nights in damp rooms and petrol-smelling vans.

And here's fragments of a notebook – yours – the oldest thing in the world of this canary yellow suit. You kept track of your travels in what used to be this book. You kept the names and numbers of girls you met once and hoped and promised to meet again on the return trip. But then you always took another route.

A black and white photograph of four young men in suits (canary yellow? It's hard to say), fags in their gobs, sideburns gripping their heads like organic motorbike helmets – Jesus, what do you look like? – this is here among these worn pages. This photo, you used to tell me, might have meant the end of your career if it'd fallen into the wrong hands – you raver you! That loutish grin you knew could charm the girls from their bedroom windows and down to the marquee was enough to guarantee the wrath of mothers anywhere. Or were those the 'wrong hands' you worried about?

So for the official snapshot, signed and laminated, the four of you stood in ascending order, left to right, smiling and looking straight into the eyes of mothers, daughters and parish priests. Butter wouldn't melt in your mouth. The sky was a tinted red behind your heads, and across it the legend *The Gossamer Showband* looked as if it might have been written by the hand of God.

But in the photo in my hand, in this photo here that

might be of myself transported back in time, I can already see the energy in your eyes that would take you nowhere. I can see the fight you and mother would have over ten bob and some backstage fling. I can see the blood on the microphone stand and the blood that would never wash out of the bass drum skin. In your eyes I can see myself lying here in this room in the future, wondering who you really were, how you forgot how to speak her name without tears, I can see myself smoking the same cigarettes as you smoked, Da, and wearing your canary yellow suit.

Everybody's Gone

Martin Meenan

Everybody's gone surfin'
Surfin' USA
Yes, everybody's gone surfin'
Surfin' USA.

It was raining, it rained frequently, not with any malice but softly, gratefully. As the moist air came off the Gulf Stream it rolled over the coast and was almost immediately required to rise over the mountains on the west coast of Ireland. As it rose it bubbled into clouds and the mountains hefted the rain onto their shoulders and it fell. The clouds, lighter, rushed inland with more exuberance. Davey stood on the side of one of those mountains, looking down at the sea. He was the son of a farmer, though farmer is perhaps too grand a word. He was the son of a smallholder, as his father had been before him, and his father before that. Sometimes when he looked up a the mountains he could feel the load of all that history, all that survival. Davey could see his father coming towards him up the rock-strewn slope. He pushed on each knee with his hands as he climbed, but was not out of breath when he arrived. He was not happy.

'Day-dreaming again, Davey?'

Davey looked again at the long beach.

'Just looking at the waves, Da.'

His father mimicked him. 'Just looking at the waves, well wave yourself over to the far field and check the stock like I told you. Christ boy, a good dog would be more use to me than you are.'

Davey was used to this, did not even know that he might feel hurt.

'I'm going now.'

Davey moved off away to a gap in the windblown hedge. As he passed through he reached into a bush and pulled out a tattered magazine. His father, exasperated,

73

shouted after him.

'And stop reading those frigging books!'

Davey had magazines in all sorts of unlikely places around the farm, he liked to read them, look at the pictures. He stole them from dentists waiting-rooms, and out of bins. Once, in an outhouse by John Molly's place, he had found a dirty one, with women in it like he had never seen before, or imagined, they seemed to him oddly deformed. He had kept it anyway, and had put a magazine on bicycle maintenance in its place. He smiled now every time he saw John furiously pedalling his bike into the village. Davey had a hierarchy of favourite magazines, and the dirty one had very quickly fallen well down the list, as the pictures had no life, no story to tell. The ones he liked best were the ones which showed faraway places and people doing exotic things. He had an old copy of *Good Housekeeping* and one of his favourite articles showed how to build and use an outdoor B.B.Q. The final picture always enthralled him, the sophisticated people standing talking in the garden, while a man in a red striped apron turned a chicken-leg on the grill. All the smiling people, the open air cooking, the safe garden, the red apron, all held a deep fascination for Davey. He had shown it once to his father, as they had sat alone in the cottage, and his father had muttered 'eejits' before scraping his plate into the brock bucket kept for the pigs. Davey had not shown his father any more after that. He was old enough now to work the farm, or help his father to. Seventeen years had ingrained the reality of his life into him as thoroughly as the soil was etched into the lines of his father's hands. Davey did not complain, he had his dreams.

When Davey reached the far field he sat down behind a dry stone wall and opened the magazine. It was his special one, he had got it from some tourists who had camped briefly on their land. He had stood beside them when he had seen them staring down at the beach, as he so often did. They were still, looking at the huge waves roll in, the smack and hiss as they hit the sand audible even at this distance. After a while they had turned away and, noticing Davey, had started talking to him. They were Americans, from

California. They were golden people, or so they had always seemed in Davey's memory. They smiled often, and hit each other playfully. They had been looking at the waves, and they told Davey that they were sure to come back to surf those rollers. They explained the thrill of riding the water to shore. They showed Davey in the magazine, *Surfing World*. They played him music on a cassette, The Beach Boys. As the words jangled out Davey could see himself, could feel the tug of the surfboard under his bare feet, could imagine the beautiful balance of it all. They had left the magazine and the cassette with him, they had not returned. He did not have a cassette player but kept the tape safe and looked at it sometimes, touched it for the magic it held. But the magazine, the magazine was different, he could look at the pictures, he could read the words. The paper became worn with use, and still the vision held its magic, Davey free, Davey moving over the waves like a god, one of the golden people, smiling with perfect teeth, smiling to the people cheering on shore, smiling at the special girl. Near to him a cow emptied itself and the splatter made him look up. He stood to look at the sea again. Why not? He had the pictures, why not ride those waves. In that moment he decided and later, when he returned to the cottage, smiled at his father and helped with new-found enthusiasm.

In the weeks that followed he began to work. He knew that he would never be able to make, let alone buy, one of the fibreglass surfboards, but he had read in the magazine how the sport had started, and how the early boards had been heavy wooden ones. He found a wide plank and marked out the shape on its surface. He did not have much spare time, but any that he had was now spent in the shed, sawing the rough corners, hacking at the plank until at last it began to take shape. Eventually his father came to the door of the shed and looked into the dusty gloom.

'What in Christ's name is that?'

'Just something, Da, keep me busy, y'know.'

'There's plenty to keep you busy, my bucko!'

'I've done all the work, I'll be in in a minute.'

His father grunted and walked away. Davey knew that

he was troubled, knew that he would have to be careful.

From his reading Davey knew that you just didn't get up on a board and surf, there was the question of balance. How could he practise that? As the board began to take shape he started to practise his balance. He walked along the tops of walls, or along the kerbstones at the side of the road. He would stand on one leg with his arms out for balance, he would sway as far as he could without falling over. Soon the local children began to follow him around and shout at him. But he didn't care, a surfer must practise. As the board neared its final shape Davey decided to make a surfing simulator. He nailed an old lorry suspension spring to a solid wooden base. On top of it he nailed another plank, which pivoted on the string and could move in any direction. At the back of this plank he nailed a crosspiece. When it was ready he called some of the children over. As Davey stood on the wobbling plank they tipped and pulled the crosspiece. The plank reared and dipped and at first Davey fell off. After a few weeks had passed he could stay on and the exertions of all the children could not dislodge him. He was pleased. His father was not, and faced him one day unexpectedly on the practise board. The children ran away in fear at the expression on his face. Davey stepped down, embarrassed at being caught.

'What the hell are you trying to do, boy, make me a laughing stock?'

'It's only a bit of fun, Da, the board's nearly finished, only one more coat of paint.'

'And then what, sail away into the sunset?'

Davey was silent.

'Your place is here, boy, on this land.'

'It doesn't hurt to dream a little, Da.'

His father seemed to groan, and hissed through gritted teeth.

'Dream, is it. Dream what dreams, waste what time, there's not time to dream Davey, and no place for it, here.'

Davey started to speak.

'It's just ...'

His father hit him then, with the switch he held in his

hand, as he would hit one of the beasts. Like a beast, hit without anger, the training of one more reluctant animal. They stood facing each other, shocked and silent. They looked into each other's eyes for the first time in their lives, and in each other's eyes saw the depths of fear and loneliness, the despair and the confusion. Eventually his father turned away and as he turned said, 'I'm burning that board in the morning, it's for your own good.'

And the boy replied, 'Yes, Da.'

Any other words would have been alien at that moment, and the words that were said were polished and easy from use.

In the early dawn the rain fell, soft as mist, as Davey carried the board down to the beach. It fell as he stripped, and as the chill tugged at his body. It fell as he lay on the board and paddled into the water. The cold shocked him, sucked at his strength, but he paddled on, further and further to where the big waves began. He turned, and in the distance, between the waves, could see the beach. It was time to stand up, to become golden. The rain fell, and everything was grey. The board slid and bucked under him as he got onto his knees, and then he was on his feet and was balancing himself with his arms. He had caught a wave and was moving, and the coldness drained him but he didn't care. The wind tore the warmth from him like rags but he was moving and looking at the beach. And then the rain stopped and the clouds parted and the sun shone. He was moving with the wave and he was smiling a perfect smile, and the beach was a long way off but he could see it all, the board-walk and the cafes and the Coca Cola sign flashing where he'd left his friends, and his girl waiting for him, proud, and smiling at him. Even over all this distance he could see her smiling, see her looking at his golden body, could see her waving through the salt spray and the tears.

In the yard of the farm there is no plank now on the spring, and the rains wash the rust from it, and it rusts again, and the rains wash it again.

Sentimental Reasons

Máiríde Woods

'I keep them for sentimental reasons,' he said, and the words with their ring of Miss Haversham still conjure up his face and that maroon Bible box, its layers of yellowed tissue-paper unfolding to reveal the plaits – sleek and fair and slightly repulsive, sunk back on their own coils like two mummified snakes.

The first time I saw them I was surprised. I watched my father sitting on the massive double bed, looking middle-aged and tired and not very Don Juanish. The plaits belonged not to some dead sweetheart, but to my father's twin sister who entered a convent, and was now ministering to the black babies. Her black and white image in the parlour was startlingly at odds with these two fair plaits.

I usedn't keep things myself. Objects were too important when I was young. I travelled light – materially and emotionally – until last year. Each time I bought a new pair of jeans, I threw out the old. And the same went for boyfriends: no relics.

Our Lady Queen of Heaven looked down on my father as he sat on that bed. The picture had belonged to his parents who had also slept in the bedroom. On the mahogany dressing-table was a red jar which held every cuff-link he had ever owned, every stray button. Beside it was a perfume atomiser in the shape of a dancing lady.

'Your aunt was a beautiful looking girl,' my father said. 'She won first prize in all the Feiseanna for harp playing. And then at the age of eighteen she gave it all up – for God.'

This bit wasn't new to me; we had been brought up on our wonderful aunt. Even my mother allowed that she had been beautiful; and she was a constant source of consolation to my father when one of us disappointed him.

My father was a disappointed man. He was eking out his life as a customs official in Ballyhooley, a village where his family had once been gentlemen proprietors. By the time Auntie Nun gave everything up for God, there wasn't much to give up, Mother implied; and by the time I was a child in the crumbling, mortgaged house, prosperity was a rose-tinted memory, a might-have-been which might have allowed my father to study music. This was what he had always wanted to do, he maintained, and learned the mouth organ to prove it.

Auntie Nun, we used to call the owner of the plaits. Her name in religion sounded like a health drink, and my parents reverted to Ella – her name when she was out in the world. Out in the world was where we were, though you wouldn't have guessed it when I was young. Ballyhooley felt like a cocoon. Everything seemed fixed, everyone knew who we were. Our father's family, fallen gentry, our mother's, go-getters with branches everywhere. On one of Auntie Nun's rare visits I remember asking her was Africa the world, and she laughed and said I'd have to see for myself.

There was a black wooden elephant on our mantelpiece which she had brought back from the Congo. It remained there even after her photograph disappeared. My parents had a soft spot for the exotic; my father treasured a cuckoo clock from Bayreuth; my mother had a bronze Infant of Prague who was dwarfed by the two flamenco dancers her sister brought back from Spain. In the kitchen hung 'A Mother's Kitchen Prayer' which I had brought back from the Gaeltacht. Every time I see it, it reminds me to steer clear of souvenirs.

I thought a lot about those plaits, fantasising about giving up everything for Christ, about the missions. I lit candles, did novenas, and endeavoured to give off an odour of sanctity. Nobody noticed much. I couldn't see any of them preserving my hair. Anyway it was too curly for plaits.

Ralph liked curly hair; and I loved his, it was so unexpectedly soft, so different from his tough guy image. The year we were together in Connecticut, I never thought of sentiment, of putting things by. Life was a continuous shining present. Being was enough; not even one day at a time, one moment at a time ... like drops of liquid in those luminous dawns, too perfect to fall.

I had fallen for Buddy Holly and paper underskirts, when I realised something had happened to Auntie Nun. A kind of frost settled over the table when anyone mentioned her name. Mother chattered about other things, and Father turned up his operatic records. And the letters stopped coming – those magnificent twelve page epistles which Father used to unfold so triumphantly from their blue envelopes, and which told us of catastrophes caused by rains and termites, of leopards and exotic ailments. We got postcards of public buildings in Nairobi. Nuns don't send postcards. Postcards are what prodigal daughters in distress send ... postcards are a cover-up. I knew something was wrong when Auntie Nun started sending them – without an envelope too. The whole village could read Auntie Nun's 'Everything's fine, don't worry.'

Ralph's last postcard was of an Indian bride holding her coil of hair. My aunt's story impressed him as an example of folk custom. When he left, everything was spelled out: how life was about moving forward and self-fulfilment, how dead relationships were like old carapaces. Americans are into communication particularly when things go wrong. We never talked much when we were happy. Why don't you love me, I wanted to cry. But the old habits of silence held. Just as well, really. He would have called me possessive and suggested therapy. We parted with no hard feelings. That way I get the odd postcard.

There were lots of hard feelings when Auntie Nun left the convent. Unspoken, of course, or only mentioned behind closed doors. I didn't know for sure until I found the maroon box tossed onto a tea-chest in our attic. At home nothing got thrown out; unwanted or sensitive items just moved to another existence in the attic awaiting disintegration or rebirth. You could reach the past by rummaging. The maroon box lay beside my graduation prospectus and Billy's Confirmation mementos, so I figured it had all happened the year I went away to university, the year I finally grew out of my family, became embarrassed by their 'Did you know Rose won a scholarship?'

I was never embarrassed by Ralph. Our relationship seemed so inevitable, as if we were two halves of an orange that had been tossed into the air and miraculously come together. But in taking happiness for granted, perhaps I didn't pay enough attention to Ralph. Not enough quality attention like the self-help manuals advise. Maybe if I had been more positive about going to L.A., maybe if I hadn't gone to South Carolina to give that course on 'Silences in the Irish Short Story' ... So many maybes.

You have to humour men, my mother said. It was her way of imparting the facts of life, but I told her that kind of thing had gone out with the stork. Nowadays it's different, I remember saying, only last summer, flaunting Ralph and my American success at her, while she sat at the kitchen table with my uncle's accounts. She had always humoured my father, dusted the maroon box, accepted his mockery of her cute brothers, kept up the house in spite of woodworm and indifferent plumbing, let him think he was doing the providing while her account-keeping put three of us through college. She had allowed him his principles and massaged our news so it didn't disappoint him unduly. Oh I saw it all. What sort of relationship is that, I almost shouted at her. But I didn't of course. She had me too well trained.

I'm not sentimental; but it was to this stone house that I returned when Ralph's absence finally sank in; when I realised that there were going to be months and maybe years like this; that the relationship I had founded my reality on was as illusory as my parents'. More so in fact; I hadn't anything I could keep for sentimental reasons, whereas my mother and father had lived out their illusions together; and even after his death, the house still breathed his presence. Ralph came from the world of mobility and replacement while I still belonged to the culture of clutter. My thirtieth birthday, my brothers and sisters marrying, made me feel different, but not in the way I had wanted.

There was a stranger in our house, an elderly lady who wore tailored suits and liked real coffee. Aunt Ella.

'Her husband died, the poor thing,' my mother said. 'Remember – the Belgian engineer ... There was all that hullabaloo with your father when she left the convent to marry him. You must remember!'

How could I remember when it had never been spoken of? But that was no excuse for my mother. She was moving house.

'This place has been too much for me for a long time,' she said. 'Your brother is going to renovate it when he gets married.'

'Aren't you sorry,' I asked her, 'leaving your things?' I hated to think of the house without my parents.

'Not at all,' she told me, 'it was always your father's house anyway. Sure I can't even remember how we came to have all this stuff.' And she put on her glasses and sat down a little stiffly to make a shopping list.

I spent the summer helping her sort things. She wasn't sentimental, but she hated waste. She left my father's books and records to me; after waging war on them for years, it pained her to be able to win so easily.

I had almost cleared the attic when I came across the maroon box. And when I opened it and saw those unchanged plaits with their musty smell, I wondered if Aunt Ella had known about them.

My mother and aunt were listening companionably to Marion Finucane as they shelled peas in the kitchen. They looked up expectantly for I had taken to bringing them any interesting relics. I opened the maroon box thinking they'd be impressed. The two plaits in the box had survived better than the hair that was out in the world, even though there was still something repulsive about them.

'My God!' my mother said. 'I thought that had gone years ago.'

'Mon Dieu,' my aunt said, 'they must be a health hazard.'

'Oh, he had Mothax in with them,' my mother replied.

Then suddenly those two old women burst into peals of laughter. My mother shook the two fair plaits out of the tissue paper and draped them over Aunt Ella's head, and as she laughed, you could see the remains of the good looks that had so mesmerised my father. It was almost as if she had been in tissue paper herself.

'Oh you were a real beauty,' my mother said. 'Whatever made you enter that convent?'

'Pride, my dear, pride,' laughed Aunt Ella. 'I thought I deserved more than Ballyhooley. Poor James,' she went on, taking off the plaits. 'He had me on a pedestal I'm afraid.'

'Sure that was the way he was,' my mother said.

The two of them wiped their eyes.

'Put those in the bin,' they told me. And I meant to. But somehow when the moment came, I saw my father's face and found myself tucking the plaits into my trunk – starting my own clutter. Some day I'll probably pass them off as my own and tell some wide-eyed child that I keep them – for sentimental reasons.

African Sanctus

Marie Hurley

Finally the train pulled out. Very slowly. Inching its way along the dust roads and burnt out bones of East Africa. Una closed her eyes, remembering the hiss of spray and rhythmic movements of the long sea voyage. An Indian ocean which had swelled up into the arms of a blue sky to deliver her wrapped in warm sun to the sticky port of Mombasa.

The heat inland had stunned her with it's waxy heaviness. 'Jambo ... Jambo ... Memsahib.' Tom was acting the idiot again. It was an old joke between them. An economics degree could not remove the remnants of Swahili from a Masai chief's son. They had been celebrating in the Nairobi Hilton after the announcement of his appointment to a London university. A gouty old colonel had staggered over and snapped. 'Boy! freshen up my whiskey will you. Pronto!'

She understood his angry frustration. Sometimes he would act out 'Uncle Tom' on the docks and frighten the more fastidious passengers. Oxbridge and a theatrical sense of the dramatic gave him that confidence. But she couldn't really blame him. Only a jaundiced eye could be cast on the assorted gimcracks exposed in the customs shed. Safari hats ... shooting sticks ... Chinese silk lampshades. 'Please have your passport, inoculation card and entry visa ready,' a customs officer would intone. He also regarded her livery of pale skin and the mode of travel with some suspicion.

'He's a Kikuyu,' Tom explained. 'He thinks you are either seriously rich ... seriously bored ... or seriously sick.'

'I'm seriously afraid,' she answered, 'of flying.' Being asthmatic was just an extra.

Disembarkation was always a slow process. Friends clustered together in groups making false promises about keeping in touch. Many of the old timers were resentful at being dragged away from silver service and afternoon tea with violins and the other pleasantries of civilised cruising.

To them, Mombasa was a lump of lard. Its white cake of harbour opened equally to taxis, buses, beggars and flies. And the non-arthritic seriously rich already had their destination mapped out. Chauffeur-driven limousines were waiting to whisk them to Malindi where wealth took the gut-wrenching heat and rolled it like marble into a pleasure dome of white sand and purple sea. And they lay anaesthetised like cats under the hot sun, sipping martinis and pretending they were part of a Graham Greene novel.

And yet, the memory of Tom she loved best was of two bear like arms wrapped around her and the welcoming hug. Inhaling the odour of vanilla and fresh coconut oil and the roughness against her skin of his strange braided electric hair. That was then.

But now, she had come to say goodbye to his ghost. To her loved one.

First a taxi to the railway station. Then the solitude of nineteenth century carriages. Separate compartments. Old fashioned, high backed rests, velvet covers, dim Victorian mirrors and overhead baggage rack.

A ticket-collector with sad eyes asked what time she would have breakfast in the dining-car next morning. She wanted nothing. Just to sleep. He fetched her a small pillow and cotton sheet and departed quietly. She switched on the overhead fan and dozed. It would take twenty-four hours in this slow train to travel 300 miles. The trip by sea, almost four weeks, could have been completed by plane in one day. But this journey was a funeral march. To honour her dead.

'Will you buy a black baby?' the nun asked. She awoke suddenly from the nightmare. Had become a schoolchild again. Saving pennies for the African Missions. The train rattled on in the early morning its gentle 'thump' over points soothing as the rocking ship she had just left.

As the engine climbed the air cooled slowly. Gradually she could breathe easier and put away the inhaler. Outside it was dawn. Antelope and giraffe stained the horizon, outline dusty as they rowed the surface brick coloured earth. Dust clouds gave a mirage effect to the flat landscape. She watched spellbound as a lumbering elephant emerged like a long forgotten dinosaur out of his invisible lair. The first day of creation unrolled gently outside the window.

And then she cried. For her two children who were cradled in her arms. Ghosts back from the grave. For her husband Tom who wanted to live here until he was an extremely old man. He was a spirit standing somewhere out there in the shadows. A god has stooped down and gathered them up in a burning cloud. And she was all alone. From the car crash she was all alone.

So she cried. For all the small villages flashing past and the years they would never share. And for all the people who would never understand. And tears ran down the glass reflection of her face all the way into Nairobi station.

'Oh my poor love,' kind Sister Rose greeted. The diminutive figure on the busy platform regarded the fragile survivor. 'You must be exhausted. I'll get a porter to load up the luggage and we'll be off.' Una wanted to tell her that this day would have been an anniversary of a different kind. Of a family finally coming home.

Ali the beggarman whose residency was just outside the railway station shuffled over. Leprosy had reduced his limbs to stumps. But he was a tough old warrior getting both disability and money from tourists. Tom was his favourite sparring partner. 'So sorry, so sorry.' The hacked face was full of compassion. She bent down and embraced him. And the old man sobbed.

'Are you all right?' Sister Rose was talking to her. Helping her into the battered jeep. Wisps of hair escaped from under the triangular veil. Gold touched her forehead and cheek in the distinctive tropical stigmata of many years' exile. Una was doubled over, almost unable to breathe. But it wasn't asthma this time. The lamentation had started. And it would continue for days. The keening. Which her Irish heart shared with this great encompassing African soul.

They were on their way to the convent. No argument. She must stay there. Not be left on her own. 'Do you want to talk?' the nun asked quietly. Una shook her head. She was like the old man. Crawling along. Carefully. Making sounds but not really speaking. Searching for words.

The school was like the top of Mount Kenya. Its snowy cowl of arched walls was pillared against the beating sun. She walked the tiled corridors and waxed pine floors. Touched and smelled the coldness of being there without him. The classrooms where she taught. The visits. His kindness ... at her fear of him and of all things African.

And then the dawning realisation of her feelings for him. On his face only horror. A little white Irish girl. It could never be. Yet a mooncrater in Africa was their oracle. It shifted and grunted a reply.

Still he hesitated. His family and tribe would disown him. He was moody. Tormented. He stayed away. Booked his flight for London. She met him at the airport with another ticket.

'You mean you would actually fly, just to talk to me?' he teased rolling his eyes. 'You would really enter one of those big metal beasts, this awesome tin bird who bellows and shrieks across the sky?'

'So now you're Lenny Henry?'

'Who?'

'Just cut the comedy.'

'OK.'

They spent six hours in the airport canteen discussing why it was all wrong, hideous, grotesque and bizarre. And then they fell in love.

And now. Alone in Nairobi. The first night of complete stillness. Away from ships or trains or engines pumping fuel into some mechanical heart ... the cicadas started their night Sanctus. A symphony of soft chirps. Lulled her to a peaceful sleep.

'Get out and talk back to this magnificent country,' Mrs Sweetman demanded at breakfast, sinking her teeth into the juicy moon shaped paw paw fruit. She scooped up some ginger with the silver spoon and sprinkled the next piece liberally. 'He would never give up. Don't you do that. And the babies. Anya and Oliver would have grown strong too. It was in their blood. The oldest tribe in East Africa. No ... let me say it.' Una had turned away. 'Each time you came back to visit I saw this. Proud and fearless. And the secret Masai

87

names that they shared. Mourn them properly.'

Down by the Great Rift Valley, the old tribe walked with their cattle or stood in groups, their long narrow limbs anointed with red ochre, ears torn loose ... intense bodies watchful. An anachronism. A protected species.

The first time she had ventured alone into the deep pit of the crater was during the monsoons. She was late returning and as visibility faded it started to rain. The thick dark cathartic downpour of the tropics turning the earth to mud.

The car skidded and the wheels spun and sunk in deeper. It would take another four hours up to the rim of the gorge. A margin at the edge of the cliff started to give way. She looked over the 5,000 foot drop to the bottom but it was just a dark chasm.

'Help, anyone,' she shouted into the storm. There was no habitation down this far into a valley which divided the continent like lobes of the brain. And this neural tissue was seismic. The place for earthquakes.

A snake had taken shelter under the car but she was less afraid of the serpent than criminals that hid out under bushes. She felt like live bait. Already her blouse and jeans were soaked. Anxiety turned to alarm as her lungs began to wheeze.

There was no medication. She checked in the car again. The inhaler was empty. Outside the baying of some animal merged with the oppressive velvet darkness of sudden equatorial night. Then the asthma slowly began to suffocate her.

She heard twigs breaking underfoot. Silence. Then a rattle and a sweeping slap against the grass. A face pressed against the window. She tried to scream but the door was wrenched open and he stood there like a giant flame illuminated by the lightning.

'Tom.' She couldn't say the word.

'Thank God you're all right.' He scooped her up in his arms. 'I've been searching since the rains started. Trees are down. The side of the valley is caving in. Let's go.'

But she couldn't talk or even walk by then so he carried her all the way. The muscles around his neck and shoulder smooth and warm and safe. Later they told her that only a Masai warrior could have tracked that dangerous edge between earth and skyline. In hospital she told him 'you saved my life. Now you are responsible for me.' Finally he believed her.

'Can you hear me Mum?' This was the 'phone call home. 'I've met someone. It's serious. We will be getting married soon and moving to London. He's taking up a university post in the autumn.'

'Oh Una ... that's wonderful.' The distance between them telescoped. Her mother got down to essentials. 'But tell me more. Is he Irish?'

A good comedian could have a field day with this farce. She was not a good comedian. Tom was the comedian. She babbled. 'Actually he is African. A real African. Black. Like Nelson Mandela. You know of him, don't you? Are you listening mother ... but he's a Catholic. Are you still there? Do you want to ring me back?'

It was an anxious pleading series of phone calls. 'You're a doctor's daughter ... laughing stock ... small town ... have you gone mad ...' Phrases that would later haunt her during the years in England when the frosty comments and the cold looks made them long again for Kenya before their children with strange accents and strange passports became tourists to their own tribe.

The government job in Kenya came through and they were packed to go when the urgent call from her mother demanded a visit. Her father was ill. 'Get a night flight Una. So the neighbours won't see you arriving. Not that I really mind. But you know how people talk.'

The dash then to the airport at midnight and suddenly the other car, a drunken driver who ran a red light. His truck lifted up the car and spun it over. She was thrown free and watched as the sky illuminated individual buildings and even other people on the street.

'Petrol tank exploded,' a bystander said. 'Keep back.'

Only minutes passed and it was darkness again.

89

Years would pass and it would still be darkness.

Now she realised that the busy Nairobi road in front of her was a temptation. Could bring about a natural conclusion to her pain. She would be squashed like an insect. Siphoned off accidentally. Like Africa. Until only the husk remained. Cars whizzed down the steep neck of the highway.

'Shall I ... I dare you.' A child again. She stood on the crest of a primitive desire ... knowing what she had become ... but not yet what she might be. A body permeable. Responsive.

A ground squirrel skidded off into the undergrowth temporarily abandoning his fixture in time, shifting the focus of her attention. She had forgotten about faith. For the first time she bent down and dug her fingers into the soil. Its skin was parchment thin from trying to grow ... sore with the effort. The tiny scrub plants were baked dry. Limbs of trees and whole trunks were amputated in places.

And yet. She inhaled. Trembled with life. Like a flower. The deep valleys were rich and perfumed ... weighed down with tropical birds. Each a small oasis feeding the dry soil with its bounty. Each part taking meaning from the other. Trying to survive. Like her ... Africa lived. She would live also.

Blood Relations

Ivy Bannister

I've put them up in a splendid hotel in Dun Laoghaire. My parents have come from California and are used to American comforts. The view from their window is spectacular. The bay is as blue as the Mediterranean, and the clouds scud overhead. With the greens and purples of Howth Head as background, it's as pretty as anything they know back home.

It's been a couple of years since I've seen my parents, and the change in my father is noticeable. But most of the time, my mother pretends that nothing is wrong. I've had a baby since I saw them last, and his cheerful antics, together with those of my older boy of ten, do much to relax things between myself and the blood relations I so rarely see.

But on the last day of my parent's visit, I can see that my mother needs time on her own. So I take my father and the baby for a walk. As we wait to cross the busy seafront road, I grip the buggy with one hand, and my father's arm with the other.

'There's nothing but red cars in this place,' he says. 'I've never seen so many red cars.'

I think, then, of the house in which I grew up, a shingled house with a great monster of a car parked in the drive. It was turquoise blue, that car, the colour of the sea in front of us.

'Daddy?' I ask. 'Do you remember the '57 Chevvy? With the tail fins and the enormous chrome front?'

The memory flickers then fades on my father's face. 'No,' he says, 'I don't remember. Was it a red car?'

'No, it was turquoise. Mom hated it.'

'Mom.' The American monosyllable sounds odd in the breeze. I look down at my baby's head. 'My kids don't call me Mom,' I say. 'They call me Mum, or Mummy.'

'Is that so?' my father says. 'What's the name of this place?'

91

'Dun Laoghaire, Daddy. We're going to walk on Dun Laoghaire Pier.'

The pier stretches over the water like an arm. We stroll along in brilliant sunshine. It's lovely for October, as if the summer doesn't want to end.

'What's the name of this place?' my father asks again.

'Dun Laoghaire.'

We stop to rest on a bench. I turn the buggy so the baby can see us. My father bats his eyes at his grandson, making a funny face, and the baby laughs aloud.

'What's the baby's name?' my father asks.

'James. The baby's name is James.'

'I knew a James once,' he says. 'He worked for the Santa Fe Railroad. I don't know what became of him.'

We get up and walk some more. Suddenly, my father begins to jog, an elderly man wobbling down the pier on shaky legs. The breeze throws back to me the notes of the tune that he's humming. They mingle in my ear with the sounds of the pier: the water lapping against stone; the chink of tackle on mast; and the whine of an outboard motor.

We sit on the broken benches at the end of the pier. We sit for a long time, gazing out across the water, and I take my knitted cap and stretch it over my father's bald head. I talk to him quietly, the place names of Dublin Bay rolling off my tongue.

Later, from the hotel carpark, I see my mother reading in a window above. 'There she is, Daddy,' I say. My father's face lights up, as he recognises her silhouette. His step quickens. He can't wait to be with her again.

I go for sandwiches, and when I return, the baby is sitting on my mother's lap, playing with her beads. My father looks down at the carpark. 'I've never seen so many red cars,' he says. 'One, two, three ...' He stops and looks at me.

'How many do you get, Daddy?'

'I don't know,' he says. 'Twenty-three! Yes, that's it. Twenty-three!' Then he frowns. 'Nope! I get seven. Seven red cars.'

When I was a kid, my father used to pay me to dig the dandelions out of our lawn. I'd lay them out on the stone wall for him to count, their yellow heads wilting among jagged leaves, roots thick like cord. I'd listen intently, as he counted, imagining the heavy coins already in my sweaty palm.

I sit my father down in the chair opposite my mother, and hand him a sandwich. 'This big thing?' he asks. 'How will I eat all this?'

I feed my baby out of the glass jar which I've warmed in the sink. He gurgles, dabbling his fingers in the bowl of the spoon.

'I know what you're thinking, Annie,' my mother says. 'You're wondering why I brought your father on this trip. I brought him to see his grandchildren. I brought him to see you. You're his only child. You don't know the effect it's had on him, your living over here.'

As my mother talks, my father chews his sandwich. 'What's the name of this place?' he asks.

'There's nothing wrong with him,' my mother says. 'It was the accident. He's got worse since the accident.'

'He shouldn't drive, Mom,' I say quietly. I hate this talking about him as if he weren't there.

'Why not?' she snaps. 'He's got as much right to drive as anyone else. The accident wasn't his fault. We were stopped at a light. I was counting my money. And then this young jerk drove smack into us, and wrecked the car. Oh Annie, you don't know what it's like to get old. It's terrible. We were like jelly for weeks afterwards.'

There's not much I can say. I spoon the last of the baby food into my child's mouth, then mop his face.

My father has finished his sandwich. He's picking the crumbs off his trousers and nibbling them. I pour some milk into a glass from the drinks tray, and hand it to him with a biscuit.

'What's the name of this place?' he asks.

'Dun Laoghaire,' I say.

'St Louis,' he says. 'That's a town in Missouri.'

'Did you hear that?' my mother says. 'He remembers

93

what he wants to remember. Believe me, I know that man inside out. He is playing games with us. He was always a devil for playing games.'

Later, I collect my older son from school, and take them all back to my house for the afternoon. I settle my father downstairs, while my mother helps put the baby down for his sleep. When we finish, I invite her to sit in my bedroom. I take a deep breath.

'What are you going to do about Daddy?' I ask.

She looks frightened. 'I don't want to talk about this.'

'We have to, Mom,' I say.

'Your father has always been a very eccentric man, Annie. It's in his blood. They were all eccentric in his family. If you think your father's peculiar, you should have known his Uncle Otto. Otto bred butterflies. In his house. You'd walk through the door, and they'd swarm all over you.'

'There's something wrong with Daddy's memory,' I say.

'You read too many newspapers, Annie. You can't open a newspaper these days without reading about that awful Alzheimer's disease. But your father doesn't have it. No way does he have it.'

'He is going to get worse, Mom.'

'Why are you doing this to me?' my mother says. Her grey eyes are filling with tears. 'You always had a nasty streak, didn't you, Annie? Remember when your Aunty Dot came to tea, and she asked where you learned to set the table so nicely? I thought you'd say that your mother taught you. But you said you'd learned at Girl Scout Camp. That was naughty of you, Annie. You'd never even been to Girl Scout Camp.'

'You need to plan ahead, Mom. If you get help now, you'll be able to cope.' But the tears are streaming down her wrinkled cheeks in earnest now. Her whole body is trembling. I feel terrible, like I've hit her, or insulted her. I see that she has enough problems, without me making her cry. The fact is, we were never able to talk properly, and it's stupid of me to think we could start now.

'I'm going downstairs,' she says with dignity. 'You can't talk to me like I'm a child. I'm your mother. Don't ever talk to me like I'm a child again.'

In the living-room, I put on a video for my parents. I go into the kitchen to help my older boy with his homework. When I look in on my parents again, my mother has gone to sleep in the armchair. I bring the duvet down from the big bed, and tuck it around her. My father is on the sofa, smoking his cigar. 'Hello,' he says.

'Howaya, Daddy.'

'This is a good cigar. What did you pay for this cigar?'

I tell him.

'You paid an arm and a leg for this cigar,' he says. 'I used to buy a good cigar for a dime.' His gaze falls upon my mother, asleep in the chair. 'Look after her,' he says. 'She is not well.'

In the kitchen I make dinner for my children. Later, I hear my mother shouting. 'Crazy old man,' she yells. 'He wants to know how many children you have!'

'Sure, Dad, don't you know that I have two kids?' I say. 'Go on. Tell me their names. You can do it. Start with the older one.'

My father looks vague.

'It's not so hard as you think,' I say. 'I named him after you.'

I drive my parents back to the hotel for dinner. In their splendid room overlooking the sea, my mother dresses. 'Blue is a good colour for evening,' she says. 'A woman should always look her best. But you don't Annie. You're eccentric, like your father. I tried to show you what was right, but you wouldn't listen. You wear terrible shoes. At your age, you shouldn't wear old lady shoes. You should show off your legs and be feminine. If I had legs like yours, I wouldn't ruin them with orthopaedic shoes.'

We go down to the dining-room, my father, myself and my mother. It's a high-ceilinged room with chandeliers and lots of pink. Everyone is old, even the waitresses, who stagger under heavy trays of ancient crockery.

My father is eyeing the menu with a worried expression. 'I can't eat all this,' he says. 'It costs too much.'

'It's included in the room,' my mother says. 'It's part of the deal your daughter arranged for us.'

'I don't like this,' he says.

'Hush up, old man, and don't spoil our last dinner with our daughter,' she says. 'God knows when we'll eat with her again. I want to enjoy my dinner. I want to enjoy myself just once before I die.'

My father settles down. He takes a key ring out of his pocket, and begins to pick at his fingernails with it.

My mother ignores him. 'Look, Annie,' she says. 'Is that who I think it is?' She shrugs delicately towards a neighbouring table.

There's an old actor who lives in Dun Laoghaire with a modest reputation abroad and a major one at home. He sits across from us now, dining alone in the pink light. Even as he eats, the actor tilts his ancient head, just so, a man who enjoys being noticed.

'Can you see what he's eating, Annie?' my mother asks. 'I want to have that too.'

I order for the three of us. My mother is happy now. I'm glad that she's found something to be happy about. It's good to see her enjoying herself. I eat with as much gusto as I can muster, and match her happy chatter with a patter of my own. Just for the moment I'm glad. Glad that she doesn't know how much worse things are going to get, before the denouement unfolds.

I Do Love You Rita Kelly

Max McGowan

I would write to you now, Rita Kelly, if I could reach you. I can almost hear you say, in that whispering voice of yours, 'O'Kelly, if you please'. Well OK, O'Kelly, Rita, but you know the Cork wit runs faster than the tongue and abbreviates everything. They say 'Paana' instead of St Patrick's Street and the 'gaza' for the street lamp and they say J.J. Carty instead of John Joe McCarthy and the 'Rockies' for Blackrock Hurling Club and 'the Well' for Sunday's Well and 'de paper' for the *Cork Examiner*.

But forgive me Rita Kelly I'm digressing. I'm in China now, would you believe? There's a frosty nip in the air. It's December in Beijing. I'm what you might call a kind of an international wandering expert. I came here on a mission for a month from Bangladesh, where it's hot and humid, and I rather like the frosty nip here. 'It's healthy,' we used to say, 'kills the bugs,' which brought me back about five decades, to you ...

I went on an official inspection tour of a sanatorium.

Walking around the grounds on the outskirts of Beijing, with a bunch of leaders (top officials to you), I was introduced to an old sea captain of seventy-six who, they said, was recovering from lung cancer. He was parchment yellow, thin, all teeth and cheerful and he said he sailed into Cork Harbour once and thought it was very beautiful. And then it all came flooding back. Almost fifty years fell away, Rita Kelly, and we were both sixteen and we had 'it', the dreaded TB, consumption, 'the bug'! I believed it had gone forever but they tell me it is making a come-back in the world again; that it is still crouching in the shadows of Asia.

It was the AIDS of our time and there was not a family in the land that was not touched by it.

In the euphemistic way of those days we were 'in a decline' they said, you and I. You remember the old sanatorium, called Mount Dessert (hope deserted you when you went there) on the Lee Road in Cork?

Now in China and in that sanatorium, today, I could see it, and you, more clearly than at any time since then. Somewhere in my hoarded archives I have a black and white photo of you and your Mam on Paana, taken by the street photographer. You had on one of the white forage hats, which were all the rage then for smart girls. And you wore high heels. They turned me on then as they do now. The Chinese girls always wear them when they dress up.

To give a photograph of yourself to a boy, without an understanding between you, was at that time tantamount to giving away your virginity. And you Rita gave me your photograph and I did not, repeat not, show it around to the lads with a nudge and a wink, 'a bit of hot stuff'. I never did, so rest easy. I showed it to my mother once and her only comment was 'beauty never boiled the pot'!

In Mount Dessert we were all laid out in serried rows on the verandah. There was some belief that only the 'good' sun rays came through the glass. We were strictly segregated, weren't we, the men and the women? The women's verandah was divided from ours by an opaque glass screen. But I had an entree. My sister, my lovely sister, had 'it' too and was in the women's section. As a special privilege I was allowed to visit her every day and that's how I met you.

Sis was confined to bed and to this day I believe she had given up the good fight and believed the nuns who said 'you would be better off praying for a happy death and your soul to heaven'. But *you* were fighting it with a saucy lust for life and you were up and about in your dressing-gown and sometimes in a dress and with your high heels. You had glorious hair and your deep-set dark eyes glowered at me, the intruder, on that first day as if I should not be there.

You needed no make up. Your cheeks were rosy, your lips ruby and your skin almost translucent.

'That's the way it is, lad,' said Reaney the old teacher from Kerry when I babbled about you in the men's ward. 'It's the glow of the consumptive. As the bug progresses the eyes get brighter, the skin translucent, the cheeks bright and glowing and the lips ruby red.' Jim Glanville, the light baritone from the Cork School of Music choir, from his bed near the window broke into:

Take a pair of sparkling eyes
Like diamonds in the skies
Take a pair of ruby lips
Take and keep them if you can
Lucky man, if you can ...

and then he broke into a spasm of coughing and had to get out his sputum bottle from under his pillow. There were red streaks in it and Jim already knew he was finished.

But I never accepted it. In spite of all the evidence I never agreed that I was ready to go. 'Only a matter of time', the quack had said, not directly to me, but he said it. I believed I could pull you and Sis through it with me. If I could beat it alone I felt anyone could do it.

When the rest moved in from the verandah in the evenings I insisted on leaving my bed outside. One of the young nuns, the one with the merry eyes, connived at it and gave me extra blankets. I often woke up in the morning with frost on them but at least I was away from the hacking and coughing and spitting and the blue sputum bottles and when they came silently in the night and took Jim Glanville's body away (hardly a week passed without two or three going from the ward) I did not have to watch it, pretending to be asleep. They all seemed to die, during the lonely night watches. Perhaps they wanted the privacy of the dark. TB patients always died quietly, causing no trouble or fuss.

'He had a beautiful peaceful death thanks be to God,' said the nuns.

But I wanted a beautiful life with you Rita and I was not specifying that it should be particularly peaceful.

You were the first great 'pash' of my life, Rita Kelly. I made many excuses to go to the women's verandah to see Sis and you. Without being boastful, I think I brightened up the lives of the women a little with a laugh and a joke. They seemed to look forward to my visits. I was sixteen, bright eyed and bushy-tailed and as long as I could see you every day I wanted no more. My jokes and fun which made the women smile were only showing off to impress you and go on, admit it, you liked it too! But you rationed me.

'You can look and admire,' you said, 'but you can't touch the goods.' You were full of those sayings, but I wanted to kiss you, long and lingering, like Clark Gable and Claudette Colbert at the 'gaffs'. Nothing sexy. You were above that in my mind. I could not even visualise sex in the same context as you. Just holding hands would be satisfying, and to intertwine our fingers, as the American soldiers did with their girlfriends, that would be ecstasy. And to just brush your lips with mine, nothing sloppy mind you, which would be tantamount to consummation, although I didn't know then what that meant.

When I lamented bitterly to the men, one day, that you were not there, when I visited and you knew I was coming, Reaney, the Kerry teacher, exploded. 'For God's sake give the girl a chance, she must get time to go for a pee, you know.' I went off old Reaney then. To associate you, Rita Kelly, with 'a pee' was to me the height of degradation.

You were there the next day, eyes laughing and your little whispering voice. You made no excuses about the day before but we made our first date.

Here as I walked around the grounds of the sanatorium, I looked in vain. But there was no turf stack. You remember the huge turf stack, as big as a barn, where we used to meet? We crept between it and the ditch and we stood facing each other and sometimes you let me hold your hands. I moved my fingers to your wrist and you said 'touch me there and you'll have to marry me', and you laughed. I know it's a cliche, but you laughed, silvery like.

'Do you love me?'

'Yes.'

'Say it then.'

'Yes ... I like your hat.'

'Me Mam said I deserved a treat and she took me into Paana and bought it for me. The nuns did not want to let me go but she kicked up a row. We had tea and cakes at the Pav and saw a film. I love my Mam.'

100

'I think you look very sophisticated in that hat.'
'What does it mean? Suff – what you said.'
'It means kind of like Claudette Colbert.'
'Go on with yeh. I'm not like Claudette Colbert.'
'You're nicer.'
'Do you love me?'
'Yes.'
'Say it then. In words.'
'Do *you* love me?'
'I won't tell you until you tell me.'

Silence. I was a virgin then and you were too. Somehow I could tell. I kissed you once, only, ever. We kept our mouths closed. We knew nothing about French kissing in those days. We did not even press hard, but we lingered. Once, only, ever, and you closed your eyes.

'I'm not coming down here anymore. If we're caught a girl could get a bad name, you know.'
'Please come tomorrow.'
'No. I'll see you on the verandah.'

You told your mother about me, too, Rita Kelly. The next day a heavy woman in black with an aggressive hat, a beak of a nose and a big handbag came looking for me. How could she have progenerated my lovely delicate Rita? I have to tell you now I thought she was a right old battle-axe!

'Keep away from her boy,' she said. 'When she gets out of here, 'tisn't the likes of you she'll want to father her children.'

We never met at the turf stack again but when I went to see Sis the next day, you whispered as we sat by the bed, 'Do you love me?' 'Yes,' I said but I could not bring myself to say the words in my head. 'I love you Rita Kelly, I adore you Rita Kelly ... I'd kiss the ground you walk on ...' But I couldn't say them Rita. I don't know why, or maybe I do but anyway to my bitter life-long regret why didn't I ... and to hell with the begrudgers.

'Write to me,' you said. 'Write me a letter and I'll write back. Me Ma said you're all lip service. Any fella who won't put it down in writing is no good.'

And I never did write it, Rita Kelly ... until now.

Now, fifty years later, I'm supposed to be a kind of consultant travelling the world and inspecting hotels and sanitoria and such like. In China TB is gone, almost, but rumour has it that once again it is waiting in the wings. I expect old Mount Dessert is silent now too, or maybe they have built a posh housing estate where the ghosts of our hopes wander.

My sister died and you died too. I survived and was upgraded to Doneraile with its two mile track through the fragrant pine woods. When you could do two circuits of the track a day you were ready to face the world again. I learned afterwards that they had actually discovered penicillin then, which would have saved you and Sis but they were keeping it for the British army.

I got out and got another chance and two bottles of Guinness a day. Would you believe Rita that I learned to drink and smoke in a TB sanatorium?

Sitting in the pine woods, another Kerryman enlightened me about women. 'The bug makes 'em passionate,' he said. 'You see, it's nature compensating. As it gets at 'em nature is telling 'em to reproduce their species. You have only to touch 'em, and they'll lep on you.' But thinking about you, Rita, I couldn't agree.

Yes I did and do love you Rita Kelly. I should have put it in writing, the day you asked me to, but I suppose I was full of boyhood inhibitions at the time and then suddenly it was too late.

Yet it's strange, isn't it, that you should have come before me today?

And, for all it's worth, I have put it in writing now. Who would have thought that day in the Cork sanatorium that I would write it in Beijing fifty years later, sitting in a cold hotel room, eight below and the only warmth, the moisture on my cold face ...? Who would have thought it?

Olly

Michael Tubridy

The kids were anti-school, anti-redneck, anti-snob, anti-police, anti-everything. 'All the rednecks have huge families, about thirty.'

They slagged each other mercilessly. Normal terms of address were, 'ya veggie', 'ya scumbag', 'ya skanger'. 'Move your feet, please', came out as, 'shift yer size twelves, ya dose-head!'

Everyone had a nickname. Elephant-eared Barry was 'Ears'. Kev, the Vietnam War fanatic, was 'Gook'. Olly, with the world's worst case of acne, was 'Pizza'.

Poor old Olly, like a photofit of a mass murderer, forever to be dismissed as a big leering lout. He'd have made a tremendous navvy; boundless energy, strong as a horse, veteran of cider parties, aged fourteen.

I didn't know it at the time, but it was on those Saturday jaunts to Glenmalure, Glenmacneas, Glen this and that, that I came closest to a group of kids. It was impossible to maintain a dignified distance crammed into a fogged-up Ford Escort, five, maybe six, teenagers yelling (they never talked, always yelled), working our way up, up into the mountains from smog and Coolock.

'O Sir Jasper ...' Mandy would screech.

'Take a hop outa the bleedin' window, you!' Kev would bawl.

I teach in a good school now, permanent post, no discipline problems, my classes get good results, but a kid never tells me his oul fella was scuttered last night and hit his Ma a few clatters.

They loved tramping over the hills, on top of the world. The worse the weather, the better the adventure. On a dismal November afternoon between Glenmacneas and the Sally Gap, we got hopelessly, miserably lost. I'd made an utter hames of using the compass and my O.S. map had degenerated into soggy bumf. Kev disappeared with a squawk down a plughole, five feet into an underground stream. We hauled him out, unharmed, waited while he squeezed pints of peaty water out of his clothes ('hate tha', Kev!'), ploughed through a young forestry plantation, waist-high in knotted vegetation, stumbling into hidden drains. Eventually we made our way onto the Military Road and slogged four miles back to the car.

The girls limped the last two miles in their socks, Mandy still singing 'O Sir Jasper ...', Sharon talking incessantly, 'O, I'd love a cuppa tea, a cup of Rosie Lee. Ah, Sewer, is it much further? D'ya know wha' I'll do when I get home? I'll have a bath ...'

'Bleedin' drown yourself when you're in it.'

'Shup, Pizza! If you'd a bath in your gaff, you wouldn't have all them poxy spots. It's dirt and filth that causes them, y'know. Then I'll watch *Eastenders* on the vidjoe. My sister said she'd tape it. I'll murder the wagon if she doesen. Ah, Sir, I'm in a heap. Is it much further?'

And that was 'the best day ever', 'a bit of a buzz'.

'Would you like to live out here?' I asked one day as we drove towards Powerscourt, thinking of their housing estates with hardly a blade of grass. 'What about that place?' A modern mansion.

There was a chorus of contempt.

'Naaa!'

'Snobby gaff!'

'There'd be no crack!'

'It'd be lonely.'

'There's no shops!'

They laughed at my attempts to slip in some poetry.

> I wandered lonely as a G I Joe, wha'
> Tha' floats on high o'er Vietnam.

'Hey, Gook, tha' one's for you!'

Wordsworth and Co. had got it all backwards.

The girls always moaned about the walking. Always.

'Ah, sir, we're not goin' up tha' big mountain, are we? Ah, Sewer, you're cruel, you are!'

'Why'd you come so?' Kev would snarl.

'Shup you! Sir, doesen he look like a ferreh?'

Bosom friends they were. They'd even started to look alike. Mandy was sunshine and showers, all charm and tantrums. Huge eyes, white face, dark hair, spindly legs. At school she was a perpetually shrieking demon who could induce migraine or early retirement in teachers. And a terrible liar. By twenty-one, I used think, she'd have bags under her eyes, be trailing a buggy and two kids through Dunnes Stores and her fella would try to beat the tantrums out of her.

Sharon was slightly less hyper. Always talking, giggling, singing. She wanted to be a model. According to Olly, she now has a job making sausages.

The first Saturday they came, the girls appeared unannounced at our pick-up point.

'What are yous doin' here?' Olly asked, disgusted.

'We're comin'.'

'Yis are not. There's no room.'

It was a blustery March day. The girls had short skirts, bare legs, slip-on shoes.

'What'll you do if it rains?' I asked.

'Geh weh,' said Mandy.

'Cry,' said Sharon.

And they shrieked with laughter, clinging to each other.

'Young ones!' said Olly.

I drove them home – they lived on the same road – gave them three minutes to change, they took twenty, the fellows blew fuses, and after that, for better or worse, Sharon and Mandy were part of the group.

Kev was like a 'ferreh' as Mandy said, a hyperactive ferret, obsessed by Vietnam. He dressed as a US Marine, was forever scrambling up trees and crags, and crawling under fallen branches. He carried a wicked-looking knife to stab rabbits and slit Vietcong throats.

'Ey, watch it, sir! There's a Gook behind tha' rock. I'll

105

toss him a grenade (mimics explosion and yells). Ey, Sir, d'ye watch *The Deerhunter* on the telly? The Russian roulette was brilliant, wasn't it?'

At some stage the girls began to pester me about bringing them all off camping during the school holidays.

'Ah, Sir, it'd be grea'.'

'What if it rained?'

'It woulden. We'd lie out in the sun in the mountains gettin' brown all over, fanny an' all ... Oh, sorry, Sir! Oh, I'm scarleh! I didn't mean tha'!'

Yes you did, Sharon.

This holiday idea did not appeal to me. Even on our Saturday excursions, I sometimes lost control of them. Notably, one day when we'd hiked to Lough Dan and sprawled in the sun eating our sandwiches and boiling a billycan.

The girls paddled, jeans rolled up, shrieked at the cold, clung to each other, overbalanced, fell with a splash, surfaced, spluttering indignantly.

'Mandy, ya wagon!' (Sharon)

'Ah, Sir, wha' am I gonna do now?' (Mandy)

'Break yer nose,' said Kev.

'Young ones!' said Olly.

They retreated behind some rocks over which, for the boys' benefit, they draped garment after garment. Then came fleeting glimpses of bare feet, arms, legs. This was too much for Kev. He tore over to the rocks, grabbed the clothes and headed for the lake. Mandy emerged at speed, mercifully in her underwear, and tackled Kev just as he tossed the clothes into the water. They both bowled over, splashing and scrabbling frantically. I dashed in, grabbed two fistfuls of hair and hauled them out. Mandy plunged away from me and viciously punched Kev's face. 'Ya pup, ya!' she spat as she cringed. Then, turning to Sharon, said, 'them young fellas have no manners,' and walked back to her boudoir with supreme dignity. For once the kids were silent before Olly said, 'Jaze, I pity the poor bloke who marries tha' young one.' And Kev, rubbing his face: 'If my Ma hears about this which threatened his hold on the imagination of the crowd. I thought I saw a glimmer of uncertainty in his face. Was it a shy face or a brazen face?

'Nothing under any of the cups,' the magician said, lifting each cup with a flourish, then replacing it smartly. He tapped each cup with the wand, twirled the wand around his thumb, then knocked over all three cups in quick succession to show a small black ball under each one.

'Three little balls from nowhere,' the magician said.

'Oh, a mighty deed!' shouted the boy.

Now I could see the heckler. A poor, thin, gawky fellow, maybe twelve years old. Despite his ugliness and shabbiness, despite his entitlement to pity, I felt an instant dislike for him as he set himself against this miracle-worker who would free us momentarily from necessity, from the rule of law, from grief. The magician continued to ignore the heckler as he dropped two of the small balls into his pocket and placed the third under a cup. He then moved the cups about until we onlookers were unsure which one had the ball beneath it.

'It's under the middle one,' shouted the boy, moving nearer the table. The magician raised the cup on the right. Nothing there.

'It's under the middle one,' shouted the boy again. The magician raised the cup on the left. Nothing.

'It's not under the middle one either,' shouted the boy.

The magician slowly raised the middle cup – smiling triumphantly as he did so – to reveal all three balls. The magician was in the ascendant now, the boy confounded. All hell broke loose then. The balls were made to disappear, reappear, transpose, and change colour until we beholders became confused, lost in the dance of the wand and the glinting arcs of the copper cups. But just as we thought that the magician was finished, that all the balls had finally flown to his pocket, that there were no more surprises, he tipped over the cups to reveal an egg under one, a tomato under another, and a lemon under the third. Only the boy did not applaud. He stood there grimly, with his arms folded, his swearing cancelled out by the applause of the rest of us.

there'll be murder, mystery and suspense.'

That day ended badly too. The kids collapsed exhausted into the car but just as I drove off, Kev summoned up enough energy to chuck Mandy's shoes out the window. She leaped out, screaming insults, and hobbled back the road to reclaim them. Foolishly, I responded to the hoots of others and cruised on. Mandy flung a shoe after us. It landed on the boot of the car. I cruised on again but stopped when I saw her in the wing mirror, utterly distraught, dancing a jig of rage. I stopped and she battered on the roof, screaming obscenities. The more the others laughed, the more demented she became. I got out to calm her but she pulled on her shoes and ran like mad yelling, 'I'm not going with yous. Yis are nuttin buh a pack a hooligans!' Sharon followed: 'Man-dy! Wa-it! Ya stupeh wag-on!' Two screaming, scrawny figures dwindling into the mist. It took half an hour to get Mandy into the car.

I remember Olly another day silently surveying Kippure and then saying, 'bleedin' bog! Why don't they do somethin' useful with it?'

'Like what?' I asked.

'Build somethin'. Grow somethin'. Somethin' useful.'

'A chemical factory?'

'It'd give some jobs, woulden it?'

'Do you not like it the way it is?'

'Ah yeah. It's a waste a' bleedin' space all the same.'

As well as the acne, Olly invariably had a black eye, a cut lip, once even, a broken nose. Whenever I commented, he laughed, 'ah, a bi' of a scrap. Ya know yerself,' and the other kids would laugh too so that I never pinned him down. Would it have made any difference? No. He was never aggressive on our outings.

I met Olly crossing O'Connell Bridge just before Christmas which brought it all back to me and made the snippet in the paper both more and less of a shock. It was four years since I'd seen him and he looked even more like a photofit of a mass murderer.

'How's it goin'?' he asked as always and as always shifted uncomfortably from foot to foot. How's the crack?'

He was 'doin' nothin',' 'on the labour'; had some news of the other kids but didn't see much of them. Asked me if I still went up the mountains.

'Not much. Sometimes,' I said.

'Jaze, I wouldn't mind doin' all tha' again,' he said. 'Best thing about that poxy school. Best days I ever had and that's a fact.'

After I'd moved jobs, he said, they'd tried to organise a camping holiday in the mountains but it fell through. Then he said 'good luck' and stalked off to set tingling the antennae of every Garda he encountered for ... what? ... another three weeks.

I'm sorry I didn't buy him a pint.

I saw the snippet in the paper by chance: 'Youth Dies in Stabbing'. Name, age, district. I rang the school to make sure. He's a younger brother there so they knew. Fight outside a pub ... stabbed in the throat ... died soon after.

So maybe our outings were the best days of his life. 'Bi' of a scrap. Ya know yerself.'

'Ah, sewer, I'm in a heap!'

'Take a hop outa the bleedin' window, you!'

'The Russian roulette was brilliant, wasn't it?'

'Shup, Pizza! If you'd a bath in your gaff, ya woulden have all all them poxy spots.'

'It's a waste a bleedin' space all the same.'

Maybe they were the best days of my life too.

Good luck, Olly.

The Illusionist

Tom Duddy

As I turned away from the doddering beggar I saw the small crowd gathered near the prismatic colours. Had I not turned away, had I paused and met the eyes of the beggar, I might not have seen the dozen or so people gathered near the silk scarf stall in the square. Indeed, I should not have been attracted anyway to a small crowd gathered in the centre of a city in which people still pause respectfully at the feet of street-musicians. But this gathering was attentive, pressed together, actively curious. And the fact that these people were gathered so close to the prismatic colours of the silk scarf stall, while yet not looking at the scarves, was eye-catching in itself. I made my way over to the gathering, glad to be distracted for even a minute or two from the sensations of grief.

Behind a small table with a green baize top stood a slight man in a dark, roomy suit. He was talking and laughing and twirling a white-tipped black wand around the thumb of his left hand. In a row on the green baize stood three cup-like vessels made of shining copper. For a moment I felt that I had stepped into the tableau vivant of an antique poster.

'One, two, three cups,' the magician said, tapping each cup with the tip of the wand. I pressed deeper into the warm humanity of the crowd, eager to see everything, to hear everything, to take in everything; eager also to be taken in, into the side-show world of colour and surprise.

'They're not cups,' a boy's voice interrupted.

'These are not modern cups, of course,' the magician went on, as if he had not heard the boy. 'These are very old cups, wine-cups, antiques. Goblets, if you like.'

'You're a bit of a goblet yourself!'

The crowd tittered, wavering between loyalty to the magician and amusement at the young heckler. The magician's eyes flickered briefly in the direction of the voice

Even before we finished applauding, the magician had taken a length of soft white rope from under the table. He took an end in each hand and proceeded to make a knot. But no sooner did the knot begin to form than a red silk scarf materialised in the closing loop. I could have sworn that it really did materialise there. As a good feeling went murmuring around the crowd the magician slid both knot and scarf off the rope and dropped the scarf on the table. He drew a pair of scissors from his pocket and brandished it as if it was a thing of beauty. In his hands it was indeed a thing of beauty as it fell into the visual company of copper, scarf and green baize. The bright blades dipped and snapped, and the magician held up two pieces of rope. 'Watch!' he said, and he threw the pieces into the air where they instantly reunited into a single length.

'You didn't cut that rope at all, you chancer!' the boy shouted.

The boy seemed older now and more menacing, the incarnation of vulgarity and philistinism. His face was flushed, his coat too tight under the arms, one point of his shirt-collar turned shabbily upwards. But the magician ignored him as he lay his length of restored rope across the table and picked up the silk scarf. He tied a knot in the scarf and held it above his head, drawing people's eyes up into the four o'clock sun. He lowered the scarf, blew gently, and the knot melted visibly away. In place of the knot (in my eyes, anyway) was the after-image of the sun.

'That wasn't a real knot at all,' the boy called out, 'it was only a trick-knot. You're only a friggin chancer.'

The magician laughed. Was it a shy laugh or a brazen laugh? I grew more irritated by the boy's heckling, his petty realism, his refusal to be cheerfully deceived. But there was nothing that I, or any of the crowd, could do. I glanced at the woman beside me, but she wasn't even looking at the magician. She was looking past me, out over the rims of her spectacles, and seemed to be focusing on a point in the sky somewhere above Richardson's pub. The man on the other side of her stepped back, glanced at his watch, and hurried away as if he had work to do, as if things like this happened

111

all the time in the city.

'Is that all you can do?' the boy asked, his eyes watery with antipathy. 'Are you finished now, hah?'

The magician was not yet visibly shaken. He did not answer but took the red silk scarf and showed it on both sides. His movements remained graceful, unhurried, artful. The square had become silent because of a lull in the traffic but it looked as if the whole centre of the city was in attendance on the magician, setting the scene for the rise and fall of the pale hands and the red scarf above the arrangement of cups, rope and wand on the green baize. As the tempo of traffic picked up again the magician pressed one end of the scarf into his closed right hand. Such deft, precise, ceremonious movements for such a banal procedure! A silk scarf being pushed into a man's fist! How could I, two weeks after the death of my father, find so much gleeful distraction in an action so pointless?

Now that the scarf was fully inside his closed hand the magician, as if raising a thurible to a deity, placed his closed hand into the irregular, chimney-ridden sky over Prospect Hill. One by one the fingers were uncurled to show that the scarf had vanished. Ah! went the crowd and I.

For a moment it seemed that the boy had been silenced. But if he was silent he was not still. His strategy of subversion had merely taken a new form. He was now mimicking the magician and doing it so well that two or three young men were sniggering away happily. The boy made exaggerated gestures with his hands, as if holding a rope and scissors, as if raising and lowering a cup, as if pushing a scarf into his fist, as if reaching into the sky and flinging open his fingers. As he mocked and parodied the magician the boy seemed close to something like glory. There were more eyes on him now than on the magician and the magician seemed to be losing control at last. The sky ought really to have darkened just a little, time ought to have stood still, the gargoyles on the Bank of Ireland ought to have spouted. But the magician was alone in the world, like his persecutor. I had great pity for the magician and desperately wanted him to regain the eye of the crowd. But his smile had become

112

broken and uncertain. Rather than continue with the battle of wills he began to put his magical objects into his black bag. As he did so the crowd began to move apart, slowly at first, hesitating and circling, looking expectantly from magician to boy. When the magician began to fold his table most of the crowd turned fully away.

'Is it all over?' the woman beside me asked.

'Looks like it,' I said.

'There's a bus at half-past,' she said, and began to walk slowly in the direction of Prospect Hill. Only myself and the boy remained.

'What do you want?' the magician asked, his face unfriendly, his voice gruff. I thought he was addressing the boy but he was actually speaking to me.

'I wanted to say how much I enjoyed the magic,' I said.

'Thank you,' he replied, his face and voice suddenly friendly again.

'Can you do real magic at all?' the boy called out. 'Can you disappear an old rag without shoving it into your fist? Can you point your finger and make a thingamajig appear in a second? Can you wave your old wand, sir, and fill anyone's pocket with money?'

'There is no such thing as real magic, sir,' the magician said, leaning on his folded table. 'Magic is lawful deception for the amusement of others, and you ruined it for everyone here today, so you did.'

'There is such a thing as real magic,' the boy said.

'Such as?'

'The priest changes bread and wine into the body and blood of Christ, our Saviour.'

'Do you see the body, though?'

'No.'

'Do you see the blood, hah?'

'No.'

The boy was disturbed. I was disturbed myself, such was the suddenness and cruelty of the blasphemous questions. I hoped that the magician would stop now, but he went on.

'As a matter of fact, the priest is a kind of magician, only

113

not such a good one. Magicians change ribbons into doves, copper coins into silver ones, torn bits of paper into flowers.' As he spoke he clapped his hands together and a bouquet of gaudy flowers sprang into view. 'And the priest,' he added, 'the priest changes the bread and wine into the body and blood – but you don't see much happen, do you, hah?'

With mock ceremony he handed one of the flowers to the boy. The boy took it as if it was a gift or a token of good-will. Now at last he was beaten. Muttering obscenities, blinking, still holding the false flower, he backed off, turned and walked quickly towards Prospect Hill.

'Did I go too far?' said the man in the dark, roomy suit as he closed the first clasp on his bag of tricks.

'No,' I lied.

'All the same, I shouldn't have made little of his beliefs,' said this man with the pale, artful hands as he pushed in the second clasp on his black bag.

'He needed to be taught a lesson,' I said.

As soon as the man with his bag of tricks started to walk towards Williamsgate Street I found myself hurrying in the opposite direction, towards Prospect Hill. I needed to find the boy, to tell him that the magician was sorry for what he had said and did not really mean those terrible things. It was important to me that the boy's belief should not be shaken. Because, although I myself no longer believe in a spiritual world, I greatly enjoy the fact that believers exist. Believers keep alive the idea of transcendence, immortality, resurrection. Believers keep alive, in my primitive heart of hearts, the idea that my father is not dead for eternity, that we may meet again some day and roam the earth together as we never did before his death. One less believer out there in the world means one less link to that incredible, magical idea.

But I never did find the poor gawky heckler. Nor did I ever see the magician again, although I'm told he sometimes performs outside Moons, especially during the festivals. The only one from that afternoon that I still bump into is the doddering beggar, that bleary-eyed bearer of the cupped and empty hand. Sometimes I give him coins, and some-times I do not. It all depends, I think, on how warmly the sun touches me in the course of its passage across the grand, phenomenal heavens.

The Skull Beneath the Skin

Barbara McKeon

It's been an odd sort of day. We had sausages for breakfast and we never get sausages on a Tuesday. Tuesday is poached egg on toast. Either they changed the routine and we'll now get poached eggs on Wednesdays instead of sausages, or someone in the kitchen has made a right cock-up of things.

Personally I don't mind. I'm very fond of both poached eggs and sausages and have no distinct preference for either a Tuesday or a Wednesday upon which to be served them. I only remark on the fact as an indication that it was the first sign that this particular Tuesday was to turn out an odd sort of day. It was nothing I could put my finger on, just a vague feeling.

After breakfast I had an appointment to see my psychiatrist. He said I was getting on great and should be out of here in no time at all. The poor man suffers psychotic delusions. There's nothing wrong with me that staying in this charming hospital for the rest of my life wouldn't cure.

Surely the fact that I want to stay in a psychiatric hospital proves I'm sick. And the fact that he wants to discharge me shows his sanity is highly questionable? He's really a kind, understanding man, too sensitive for this job. He should be an animal keeper in Dublin Zoo. Cleaning up after the elephants is more his line. The only mess they make can be used on his rhubarb. What use can he make of the mess my life is in?

The woman in the room next to mine had to go for shock therapy this morning after breakfast. Not that they gave her any breakfast, so the conundrum over sausages or poached eggs is purely academic to her. And not that she'd have cared. Mrs Mallory has a severe problem with depression. Chronically depressed she is. There's no life in her, she's

116

miserable and mopes round the place all day and half the night. At least her husband sticks by her, which is more than mine did.

Anyway, Mrs Mallory was brought down in her dressing gown and slippers by two nurses walking on either side. My heart went out to her going for ECT, but she was miles away, like she was pushing a trolley down an aisle in Quinnsworth. She had been sedated and would be anaesthetised before they released a wallop of electricity through her brain. The gas thing is, you don't feel a thing. And funnier still, the doctors don't actually know why it works, only that it does.

I wouldn't like it myself. I'm not manic depressive, I'm just mildly off my rocker. But if I felt a bit of mania coming on I'd stick my finger in the electric socket and perform a do-it-yourself job.

When I next saw Mrs Mallory, which was at lunch, she was all dressed up and seated at the table with five other patients regaling them with all sorts of chit chat like she hadn't seen civilisation for a decade. In a way she hadn't, being locked up in a depression for all those years. A few more sessions of galvanising her brain cells and she'll be right as rain.

Ructions broke out on one of the male wards when it was discovered one of the patients on the alcoholism programme was having drink sneaked in by his girlfriend. It was ingenious. She'd buy a dozen oranges and inject vodka into them. So there was your man sucking an innocent Mediterranean citrus fruit and getting plastered into the bargain. He's been given his final warning. My God, it'd make you nervous about buying a packet of wine gums.

We had a lecture after lunch and in the middle of the counsellor's dissertation on how alcohol affects the liver as proved in tests on two perfectly harmless and previously teetotal laboratory rats, the projector took a seizure and broke down.

Then a gentleman jumped to his feet and berated the counsellor for approving of experimenting on animals, whereby the lecture became an unintentional victory for

117

anti-vivisectionists. I agree with them, why should animals suffer because of the way we humans abuse our bodies. Rats don't expect us to live in sewers, why should we expect them to drink pints?

I wonder what my psychiatrist would say if he knew I had an erotic dream about him last night. He's not my type, but then my type has never been any good for me anyway. Witness one husband gone AWOL. He wasn't the only one, and the thing is it's always happening. Every time I fall in love I think this is the real thing. I've had the real thing so often I could be a bloody Coca Cola company.

I'm not saying I've fallen for my shrink, I'm only saying I had a vivid dream where he and I were, you know, doing it in his consulting-room. When I sat in the chair opposite him this morning I could hardly keep a straight face. There he is thinking I'm recovering from my breakdown and there's me visualising him naked down on the floor. And he wasn't laying the carpet. Pity it was only a dream.

Dr Chambers never tells me I'm useless, he tries to build up my confidence, not tear it down like that bastard husband of mine used to do until he cleared off on me and the kids with that bitch he'd been screwing for the last six months. Is it any wonder my hormones started hallucinating when someone pays me a bit of understanding?

Mrs Mallory isn't in my group so I didn't see her again until tea-time. There she was once more presiding over her table like a viceroy over a colony. Sitting beside her was Billy, a handsome, intelligent man who said if she wanted to join the carpentry class he'd be happy to let her use his tools. Everybody screeched laughing at his unintentional double entendre, as Billy is a priest.

This place is dense with clergy and it's amazing to discover how human they are. It's bad enough to have to admit you're an alcoholic or a drug addict or suffer mental illness without having to announce you're a priest or a nun too. Housewives who go loopy are utterly commonplace. I'd invent a connection with royalty only it's likely everyone would believe me.

There's a very nice mix of people in this hospital. We sit

118

down to our evening meal in groups of six at about ten or twelve tables in a colour coordinated dining-room. We could be at a Rotary Club dinner. At my table there is an accountant, a sales executive, me a housewife, a university student, an alcoholic psychiatric nurse (maybe mental illness is contagious) and a stunningly beautiful girl who suffers from an anorexic condition.

Angela has defeated the doctors. She will eat food only of a certain colour. This week it's green. It's no use dyeing her mashed spuds the colour of cabbage, though it's been tried. So while we have poached salmon (we're all private patients on VHI), Angela has a plate piled high with spinach, peas and broccoli.

When she is served food of the wrong colour she shares it out among the others at the table. They usually decline. Taking food from an anorexic is like helping her write her suicide note. So she puts the offending cuisine in her handbag so the nurses won't see she hasn't eaten it. She's taken more food out of this dining-room in her handbag than the rest of us take out in our bellies.

I don't know. They should have a sign on the wall like you see in offices: 'You don't have to be mad to be here, but it helps'.

After the meal I played a game of pool with Billy the priest. He's a fine thing. A good-looking man and a nice person. What a pity he's celibate. What am I talking about, so am I and I'm married. My mother is minding the kids while I'm in here. They are the only reason I would want to leave. Plus the fact the VHI will run out some time.

Why would I want to leave? I'm happier here than I've ever been. My husband thinks I'm too fat and my children think I'm the maid. I studied economics and political science at college and end up an authority on washing powders. So he runs off with his skinny blonde tax consultant and I have a nervous breakdown. Well, I may have been broken but I will grow again, stronger than before. I will not be everybody's doormat, I will be true to me. People here like me for who I am. They helped me find myself again. Crazy, isn't it, that it's the patients of a mental hospital who showed me how to stay sane.

And of course Dr Chambers, to whom I tell everything; things I never told anyone else, the pain, the fears, the loneliness. He listens, encouraging me to open up and exorcising the goblins with psychiatry. Except I don't think I'll tell him about last night's dream. It'll only drive the man wild with desire.

Just before I was going to bed there was a phone call for me. It was my husband but I didn't want to speak to him. I asked the nurse to take the call. She was on the phone quite a while, not saying much but nodding her head and saying 'yes, yes,' sympathetically.

I wondered what was up but I couldn't bring myself to go to the phone. I sat in my room with the door open and waited for Nurse Collins to come back. That vague feeling of apprehension crept back into my bones. I had my make-up off by the time the call was finished. The night nurse had also been around and given me my lithium and anti-depressants. I felt like asking her for a stiff brandy.

Nurse Collins tapped on the door. You could see she didn't quite know how to word what she had to say. Yes, yes, she said to my anxious enquiries that the children were all right. So was my husband, and my parents, and his parents, and everybody else on the entire road for that matter. So who was hurt or sick or broke or whatever?

'It's your husband's ... er ...' stammered the nurse.

'His girlfriend?' I said helpfully.

'Yes, I'm afraid there was an accident. Her car collided with a truck and she was killed outright. She's dead, I'm afraid.'

Did you ever get news that you didn't know how to react to? It seemed churlish to yell yippee! though part of me wanted to. When the nurse closed my door I did a little celebratory dance around the room. I let a few silent yahoos hit the ceiling and beat my fists off an invisible drum. Then I sat down as all the feeling seemed to drain out of me. I felt weak, it was like being hit with a brick. At first I was stunned, then the pain came. My skull seemed to crack open, the tears ran like blood and I just cried, and cried, and cried.

The Last Butterfly

Alan Titley

It was my last summer before I went to secondary school. If it wasn't, it was certainly the last summer I spent with my brother as the following year he went off to work in Tramore on the roundabouts. We were staying with my Aunt at Cool-feakle and she was as changeable as the clouds. But she did let us wander at will through the fields and meadows as long as we fetched water from the well. I thought she kept a cobweb on her head until Martin told me it was a hairnet she wore to keep her hair from going grey. I never knew when he was joking or not.

We had picked mushrooms in the morning because it had been damp, and Auntie fried them with buttered pota-toes and cabbage for dinner. They were things I would never eat at home but hours rambling through the fields with the wind at my back and the grass under my feet would give you an appetite for old boots. The sun came out while we ate and I could see Auntie smile at it as if she knew something that it did not.

'Not before time, either,' she said, as she shuffled back to the dresser for a side plate.

'I suppose it'll shine all the time tomorrow,' Martin said. 'Just after we get the train.'

'And it'll blaze when we go back to school,' I chimed in, showing I could be as pessimistic as the rest.

'Don't moan,' Auntie said, but not severely. 'Moaning never stopped the rain. Did you never hear that?'

We didn't answer as we didn't want another long gabble about the weather. It amazed me how grown-ups could go on and on about the weather as if it really mattered. My motto was if you didn't like the weather just wait a while and it would change.

'I think I'll catch ladybirds,' I said after we had put our dishes in the basin, but I didn't get any response from

121

Martin.

He came with me nonetheless. We went through the potter's field and up past the Bracken Glen and round by Maggie Maurice's old house which was now deserted since she was taken away and out as far as Aughinish. We could see the sea from there sucking the gentle heat from the sun and rolling round the rocks to the shore. I hadn't caught any ladybirds yet but I still had my jam-jar.

A fly went by with a hum in it but who wants to catch a fly?

Martin said, 'This is boring.'

I didn't think so because I liked the sea and sky and the green fields that were everywhere and laid themselves out in all directions. Sometimes I wished I could just run and run and run and run away over the horizon and throw kisses at the wheat and the corn and smell everything as it is first thing in the morning. There were times when I would love to be a scarecrow but that was a secret I would never tell anybody.

'Look, look at them,' Martin said, grabbing me by the arm and pointing my eyes towards Muckers' Acre.

I didn't see anything unusual but Martin seemed intent on showing me anyway. There was the field and some hay-stacks and a man and another person near the gate. He was wearing a bright red and yellow anorak which reminded me of fried eggs and tomato ketchup. His size shadowed the other person and it wasn't until they began to climb over the gate that I saw it was a woman. She wore a green headscarf the colour of cooking apples of the kind that are too bitter for even Auntie's tarts.

'Come on, let's follow them,' Martin said.

'What for?'

'It might be fun.'

'I want to collect ladybirds.'

'You're a sissy.'

'You're silly.'

'Maybe they're spies.'

'There's nothing round here to spy on.'

'Oh yes there is. The Relihans' house was broken into

122

last week and they know it was sussed out first. I bet you that's what they're up to. Why else would they be going through the fields and not by the road?'

I couldn't answer that so I tagged on behind. Martin kicked the thistles as if they were footballs but I preferred to leave them standing. Anyway, most of them just jumped back up as if he was wasting his time. I thought time was there to be wasted but Martin was the one who always wanted to be doing something.

We stayed at least a field behind and they were making very slow progress. Maybe they were noticing everything like Martin said as spies and robbers have to notice everything. We also had to stay out of sight and we picked blackberries from the bushes. I wouldn't let him use my jar to collect them as I detested blackberry jam and knew what I wanted it for.

'Think Auntie will kill us if we come home with wet feet?' I asked, as we were going through a soggy dip towards a stream.

'Who cares?' Martin said. 'We're going home tomorrow. Ma won't mind. She'll be washing all our clothes anyhow.'

'I like it here,' I said. 'I think I'd like to live in the country when I grow up. It's big. It's wild.'

'It's boring.'

Martin thought everything was boring apart from his crummy records. He'd listen to the same song for hours and discuss it with his pals. I think Ma sent him down the country just for a bit of peace.

We were trailing along beside the stream on the way to Berwick's Wood when I saw it.

It floated out from underneath a tall fern and moved on to a ray of sunlight. It had the most beautiful black wings I had ever seen and they were tinged with red like jam through a doughnut.

I could not tell one kind of butterfly from another but I knew that this one was special. It flitted in and out of the sunlight as if it were preening itself and more than anything else in the world I just wanted to stay in that spot and admire it.

'Look, Martin! Look!' I whispered, fearing that any loud voice would frighten it away.

Martin looked back and cast one eye on it. 'Yes, it's a butterfly or a moth or something. It's lovely. Now come on.'

'Just a minute,' I said, 'I want to look at it.'

It moved across the stream as if on a ferry of sundust and just as I was about to wave it goodbye it alighted on a thin reed which jutted out from the bank. It appeared even more beautiful when at rest and I stepped out onto the stones to get a closer look.

I could not believe my luck when it didn't fly away. I stretched out my hand breathlessly and yet it did not move. The black was lovely, lovely like the mouth of a cave and the red was as the dawn coming through it. I could have prayed that it would never move and that I could stay there watching it more beautiful than all its surroundings for ever.

I heard Martin shouting at me from up the stream. He seemed miles away but somehow I didn't care. He shouted again more angrily this time and I knew I would have to leave. Quickly, without thinking I stretched out the jam-jar and enclosed my butterfly under the lid. Thankfully he could make no sound as I did not wish to hurt it in any way and I knew that I would soon let it go.

'Hurry up! What's keeping you? We've lost them.'

I tried to show him my black beauty but he wasn't interested. He just kept pushing ahead through the scrub and yapping at me to move it.

'Damn it,' he said as our rough path forked out from the edge of the stream towards the wood. 'Because of you we'll never know which way they went. You've blown it.'

'Maybe they left a clue,' I said, hoping I might have said the right thing. 'Maybe we'll find a piece of cloth on a bush.'

'Rubbish,' he said, pushing ahead. 'We'll just have to go one way and take a chance we're right.'

I followed him faithfully through the wood even pretending to hide behind the trees as he did. Every so often I got a chance to look at my butterfly and he would gently flit his wings at me. The brambles that coiled out to ambush us didn't seem to bother Martin and I wouldn't have minded if he didn't let them snap back on me. I don't think he even noticed.

We had been walking up a hill for some time when the trees began to thin out. We came to a barbed wire fence but the path turned and ran along beside it. There were very few trees on the other side of the fence and Martin said we should go through as we would get a better view and might spot them. We moved further along the path to try to find the opening when I saw the green scarf caught on the wire.

'Come on,' Martin urged, and I went through first and then held the wire up for him as he was bigger.

We ran along the grass margin of trees and then up the hill again as if we were on a treasure hunt. I'm not sure where we went after that as I just followed Martin as he ran and crouched and zig-zagged and ducked through the ferns and bushes until we came to the lane.

'I hope this leads on to the road,' I said. 'I'm tired.'

'Come on,' he said, and I followed.

The lane ran right up to a high wall with a big wooden door cold in the middle. It was closed. We pushed but it would not open.

'What do we do now,' I said, 'go all the way back?'

'Give me a leg up,' Martin said, as he tried to get a foothold in the wall. I helped him and he managed to hoist himself up far enough to see over.

'What is it?' I asked, 'what's there?'

'Nothing much only another big field.'

'Well come on then.'

'Just a minute. I'll be down in a minute.'

'Give me a hand so.'

'There's no need. It's nothing. Just a field.'

'Must be a great view if you ask me.'

When he did come down I thought he was angry with me. He said nothing for a while but just strode away back towards the hill which seemed much higher now. I found it more difficult to keep up with him this time and I knew it was a long way home.

'What's that you have in the jar?' he asked suddenly.

'It's my butterfly,' I said. 'Don't you remember?'

'Show it to me.'

He glanced at it briefly and what looked like a smile appeared on his lips.

'Silly girlish stuff,' he sneered, as he opened the jam-jar and rolled my beautiful butterfly between the palms of his hands.

All I ever remembered then was the black powder falling and the fleck of red on his fingernails.

Wasps

Joe O'Donnell

Eventually I had to admit that she was right. There was a buzzing. And it did seem to be in the attic. Or the unfinished attic.

For days she'd been saying: 'There's something up there. Some insect or bee or something trapped. I can hear the buzzing.'

For days I'd doubted. But that night it made itself heard. A low buzzing. More hum really than buzz. I promised I'd have a look at it in the morning. Our attic, or what we refer to as the attic is rather difficult to get into.

It's really no more than a trap door in the ceiling. Nailed shut this – what? – six months, eight. No, ten months. We were getting the attic converted. The time grants were available, everybody was getting an attic conversion.

Moira had just had Jennifer, our first baby. The baby was eight months old. That's it. It was ten months ago.

The builders had moved in. Two young strong lads who made a hole in the ceiling and created noisy havoc for a few days. Except when they had their tea break. Then one of them, we never knew which one, would play slow airs on a tin whistle. That's the thing I remember about that time. The slow airs.

Of course, the only reason I remember that was because Jennifer died. The baby died: just like that. I mean, literally just like that. Cot death. Inexplicable, they told us. No real explanation, they said. And most certainly nothing to blame yourself with. They said.

We stopped the builders. They were most under-standing. Said they'd come back whenever we decided. They put a trap door on the unfinished conversion.

And nailed it shut.

Funny thing that. I hadn't thought of it for some time now. Of course you never forget. Not something like that.

127

Ever. But I hadn't really thought about it until Moira said. About the wasps.

Then I could almost hear that tin whistle. And the bang of the hammers. The buzz and whine of their power drills seemed to have returned.

In the night.

A droning carpet on the threshold of sleep, ready to be pulled from under you, ready to tip you headlong into a nightmare.

Morning. I pulled the steps in from the garage and lined them up under the trap door.

'Probably a couple of wasps got themselves caught there,' I said.

Armed with a torch and a claw hammer I went up the steps. I'm not the greatest one for going up a ladder, any ladder. I feel particularly vulnerable. Steps make me feel unsteady, especially if I've anything in my hands – a shears, a paint brush, or in this case a hammer and a rubber cased torch.

The nails did not come out easily. Moira held the end of the steps as I yanked them. They squeaked out reluctantly. Good six inch nails. The heads painted over with the ceiling paint, the shanks still silver shiny after their ten months interment.

The trap door was hinged crudely at one side. The paint had hardened along the edges and I had to use my elbows and the full weight of the hammer to bang the trap door up.

Suddenly it gave and I faced a large open space. For only one minute. I think what startled me was the sudden rush of sound. That's the only way to describe it. A cataract of buzzing poured from the black gap. The darkness was alive and palpable. It startled me and I hauled it shut. I looked down to say something to Moira.

Her face, upturned, shocked, pale.

I scrambled down the ladder and put my arms around her. She was trembling.

'It's okay, love, okay.'

'What is it?' she whispered hoarsely.

'Seems to be quite a few of them up there – a lot actually.

128

I'll have another look.'

Moira clung to me.

'I'll be very careful,' I said, 'very careful.'

I climbed the ladder and gently eased the trap up an inch or two. This time more than sound poured from the trap: wasps swirled through the opening. I dropped the trap and jumped off the ladder. Moira was already beating them away. Those that didn't escape, we killed.

Over a cup of coffee we took stock. There was no question but that wasps had taken up residence in our unfinished attic. It didn't take long to find out how they got in. Outside over the boiler house there was a crack under the gutter, host to the goings and comings of an endless stream of wasps, hell bent on God alone knows what sort of business.

The Yellow Pages had four and a half columns of pest exterminators, between the Personal Development Courses on page 542 and Pet Foods on page 544. We picked one at random. 'Though it wasn't quite random: we were impressed by the drawings on the display advertisement which showed hooded and gowned operatives with hi-tech backpacks.

They offered quick clean extermination without fuss. The twenty pound fee didn't seem excessive. I agreed and was assured that their 'team' would be with us by half past six Monday evening.

It was a long weekend. Moira quiet, scared of passing down the hall under the trap door. I tried to make jokes. Rapping at the trap door from time to time. 'Hey you guys, start saying your prayers, your hours are numbered.'

Sunday evening I watched from outside. Over the boiler house the activity was endless. In and out. Endless.

Moira who had gone into herself somewhat since Jennifer died seemed now to have pulled the trap door shut. She scarcely spoke for seventy-two hours.

We waited on Monday. Like children. Would the exterminators arrive in a heavily plated armoured vehicle? Descending with a cumbersome gait, encased in silver grey space suits, heavy boots and with chrome-silver gas tanks strapped to their backs.

Would they ask us to leave the house? To return in an hour or two?

About ten minutes later a battered Volvo drove up and a heavily built man wheezed himself onto the pavement. He wore a shabby grey suit with a tight waistcoat. He introduced himself, borrowed my torch, and my step ladder and cautiously lifted the trap.

He poked his head in, shone the torch, lazily batted off a dozen wasps who stormed out and then slammed it shut.

'Jasus, missus,' he said to Moira, 'you've the full lash there and no mistake.'

'Will it be difficult?' I asked. I was thinking that maybe this was merely a preliminary inspection. That now he knew the extent of our problem he would ring up base and tell them to bring in the heavy equipment.

'Not at all,' he said. 'Just it's one 'a the biggest I've seen. Now would you have a long bamboo stick, or maybe a broom handle, a piece of sticky tape and a match?'

Moira got the bamboo stick: six foot long from the French Beans in the back garden. I got the sticky tape, and a pack of book matches which said El Capistrano Villages, Nerja, Malaga. We'd been there on holiday once. That's where we started the baby, I reckon. Neither of us smoked now.

I tried one of the matches. It sent a sliver of sulphurous smoke to the ceiling.

He took two inches of sticky tape, broke it off with a dirty thumb nail and parked it on the back of his hand. Then delicately he removed a tiny purple tablet from his waistcoat pocket. We both watched in silence as he placed the tablet on the tip of the cane, and fixed it in place with the sticky tape. The only sound was of his wheezes.

'Nearly there,' he smiled at us. He held out his hand. 'Match.'

'Pardon?' I said.

'Match,' he said, 'to light it.'

I gave him the book of matches. He handed me the bamboo and eased himself up the ladder. It groaned under his bulk.

'Now when I give the word, hand me the stick and get out of the way. Just in case of any accidents.'

He broke off one of the matches and cracked it with his thumb. He applied it to the purple tablet. The match went out. He lit another. This time the tablet caught. With a hiss it erupted smoke like a tiny volcano.

'Now,' he said.

Dropping the matches, he grabbed the stick, pushed the trap door up and hauled himself into the attic. The door shut behind him. We looked at one another for a moment, then ran into the kitchen and slammed the door. We listened. Not a sound.

'He's mad,' I said, 'stone hatchet mad. The little buggers'll sting him to death.'

'If ... if anything does happen,' said Moira, 'how are we going to get him down? He's a big man.'

Then we heard a loud coughing and spluttering. We poked our heads out of the kitchen. The exterminator was crawling down the ladder, eyes streaming. 'Oh Jasus!' he said and slumped beside the wall, ashen faced. We stood looking at him.

'Can we get you something?' asked Moira.

'Are you all right?' from me.

He waved his hand. Eventually the words came out in wheezy gasps.

'No problem, no problem, squire. Could I have a glass of water. Be okey-dokey in a minute.'

He sipped the water, then rose to his feet.

'Sorry about that. Hope it didn't startle you. Getting a bit old for this job I think. Now what was the quotation? Twenty pounds I think?'

He had a receipt made out. It was rubber stamped with the name of the firm and signed with a scrawl.

'The ... eh ... you know ... up above?' I pointed to the trap door.

'Give it a couple of hours, then you can clean out the nest. A big one. You can burn it, or put it in the bin. You won't have any more trouble with them lads this year. Sometimes they come back the following year. But that's next year and another day's work, eh?'

He left. The attic was silent. After two hours I went cautiously up through the trap door. The flash lamp revealed all. I called Moira. She wouldn't come up.

Wasps lay in their thousands. Dead. There was a sweetish smell in the air. Like the stuff you put in drawers to keep clothes fresh. But over in the corner hung the nest. Unbelievable. Big as a rugby ball. I broke it off at the stem and carried it down.

We looked at it in awe. It was truly an amazing construction. Made of something that looked like paper, but not like any paper we'd ever seen. Thousands of tiny hexagonal combs all identical in size and structure and fitted together meticulously. We carried it out to the back garden. It was quite solid. I broke it open with a spade.

There inside were hundreds of tiny pale bodies, grubs and partly formed wasps. Dead.

Quickly I poured petrol over it and set it alight. It burned for a long time. I couldn't take my eyes off it. Then I heard it: the weeping.

Moira was behind me. Sobbing. I put my arms around her. I knew she was thinking of Jennifer. I had already wept. Lots. Moira hadn't. We walked back into the house like a pair of mutually supporting convalescents.

Later over tea: 'I think it's high time we got that attic finished. Do you remember those two guys? What were their names? I'm sure I wrote them down. Wonder are they still in business? Wonder does your man still play the tin whistle?'

I was rabbiting on. The wasps were dead. The way ahead seemed clear now. And possible.

Nicaraguan Coffee

Joe O'Donnell

'Just Dorothy?' I said. 'I mean, do I call her Sister Dorothy or what?'

'No,' he said, 'that's her real name. That's what I'm going to call her anyway.'

'Well, you're different,' I said. 'I mean, your relationship is different for a start.'

'What relationship?' he said. 'That was twenty years ago.'

I'm not normally that niggly. I mean, it's his style, isn't it. Never let your right hand know what your left hand, etcetera, etcetera. And in our eighteen years of marriage he'd sprung many surprises on me. Friends out of the blue, business acquaintances. At the drop of a hat.

I had coped. I was good at it. Good at putting together a meal from whatever was there without having to apologise for it. Others might have baulked at it. I accept it as a challenge.

I'd read in a book once that problems and challenges are the same: it's how you look at them that matters. And that had had a profound influence upon my life. Subsequently.

So why had I doubts about this one? I mean I know the question of how to address the particular lady was a trivial one, to say the least. I wasn't really worried about that. I take people as they come.

But there was something else. I think it was the ... vagueness? Is there such a word, vagueness? I think it was the way he said to me: 'Oh Dorothy rang me the other day. I invited her 'round for dinner. Saturday. Saturday, okay with you?'

I mean he would normally have said something like: 'I've invited Jackie 'round for dinner on Saturday. Jackie's the new guy in Data Processing. Did time in Harvard. Still a bit wet behind the ears, 'though he seems to have a fair amount between them. Camp, but clean. Doesn't know

133

many people here yet.'

That sort of thing. To fill me in.

But Dorothy. Just Dorothy.

Of course, I had asked: 'and who's Dorothy when she's at home?' And he said: 'Dorothy ... you know. The girl who went on to become a nun.'

'Oh that Dorothy,' I said.

I had never met that Dorothy. She was before my time. But once I had come across a snap in the back cover of one of his books when I was dusting them. It was one of those black and white pictures taken by a street photographer on O'Connell Street outside the Gresham Hotel sometime in the sixties. She was thin and beaded and head-banded. He had a beard. He doesn't wear one now. Hasn't done so for ... well, a long time. In the picture he had his hands stuffed deep in his jeans; she was linking him with both hands, her head tight to his shoulder. She was very beautiful. The photograph reminded me of something. I couldn't remember what at the time.

'Who's the one?' I asked him.

'Oh, that's Dorothy,' he said. 'Just a girl I knocked around with. Long time ago.'

I put the photograph back where I found it. He must have taken it out later. Because the next time I checked, it was gone.

Dorothy was a girl to whom he had once been engaged. Or sort of engaged. Or nearly engaged. I was never sure.

Then something happened and Dorothy went off and joined a convent. The Dominicans. The long white robes would have suited her. Down to the ground. She had the height and style to carry off robey things.

She was most certainly not wearing a robey thing on the Saturday night. Nor anything like it. I got the shock of my life when I answered the door. She was older, but still beautiful. She wore a tight fitting black dress: simple, direct and elegant with a tiny black beaded Victorian bag and good shoes. Oxfam, I thought. But Oxfam with style.

It was the contrast that threw me for a moment: long white robe, short black dress. But you never know nowadays, do you? Most of them wear casual clothes when they're off duty, so to speak.

'I'm Dorothy,' she said.

Her handshake was firm and dry. All of a sudden, mine wasn't. She brought a gift for me: a small and delicately carved wooden spoon.

'It's native craft work,' she explained.

I didn't doubt it for a minute.

I had been afraid that conversation at dinner might be sticky. It was anything but. Of course there were times when I got a bit out of my depth but I thought I kept my end up. I'm no ding-a-ling and I do read *The Economist* and *New Society*.

I was mad keen to bring the conversation 'round to religion, just to get her talking about being a nun and maybe making her feel more at home. But he wasn't interested. Neither was she it seemed.

We talked about the recent Shakespeare at the Gaiety. And how Kenneth Branagh was stunning. We'd seen all three plays. She only saw *As you Like it*. We talked how Ken Russell in his recent TV Omnibus had put the knife well and truly into Michael Tippett. I said something about Elgar's Enigma Variations which made everybody laugh. Everything was going well when I served the coffee and After Eights.

He had brought home some Nicaraguan coffee on the Saturday afternoon. Had to travel into Dublin to get it from some health store in Temple Bar. I had bought Bewley's decaffeinated. That has been his coffee since his heart thing last year. It's a good coffee but this time nothing would suit him but Nicaraguan.

'Why?' I asked him.

He smiled. Shrugged. 'Just for a change,' he said.

'Is it decaff?' I asked.

'It's not really important,' he said.

'It was bloody important a year ago,' I was going to say, but then: every problem is a challenge. And for all I knew then, it wasn't important. He gets figaries.

She recognised the coffee. She smiled at him.

135

'Just to mark the occasion,' he said.

I felt left out for the first time that evening. It must have shown because she turned to me and explained.

'I was in Nicaragua,' she said.

She said Nicaragua in a way that made it sound foreign, which in a way it is. The way some Americans have of saying *Viet Nam* as though it were *Viet Nom*.

'Were you on the missions?' I asked.

'In a manner of speaking,' she said. 'We were working with the people. People who could have produced this very coffee. That's why it's important that people buy it. It's more than coffee. In a way, it's a political statement.'

I laughed at him. 'There now,' I said, 'I was making political statements, when I thought I was only making coffee.'

'Talking of political statements,' she said to him, 'do you still have the Bob Dylan records?'

He told her that they were somewhere out in the garage. He offered to get them. She said she'd help him. I said I'd stay. Make more coffee.

They went off to the garage. As they were going out I heard him tell her that he hadn't played them in about five years. He didn't tell her that he had cleared them out about ten years ago. He had quoted Saint Paul then. Something on the lines of 'When I became a man I put away childish things'. That's what he said then.

They came back with an armful of dusty LPs. I knew the titles. *The Times They Are A Changin'*, *Highway 61 Revisited*, and *Bringing It All Back Home*. As well as *The Freewheelin' Bob Dylan* which had a picture of a couple walking down a city street.

I remembered now what that photograph had reminded me of. Dylan has his hands stuffed deep in his jeans; she links him with both hands, her head tight to his shoulder. She is very beautiful.

As he shuffled the records onto the turntable I said: 'maybe Sister Dorothy would like another cup.'

There was an uneasy pause. She looked at him, with a whimsical smile. He pursed his lips and shrugged.

I looked from one to the other.

136

She took my hands, my sweaty hands, in her hard, dry ones.

'I'm sorry,' she said. 'It's just the Sister Dorothy bit. You see, I left the Order about six years ago.'

He shook his head. 'That's a good one,' he said, 'Sister Dorothy. Hah.'

He dropped the stylus on 'Don't Think Twice, It's All Right'.

I think it was at that precise moment I knew there was something between them. We sat through an hour of Bob Dylan. I don't think I heard a single note or word he sang. We drank some more coffee. We didn't say much. There really didn't seem to be much more to say. She left, promising to be in touch soon.

When he returned from seeing her to her little Deux Chevaux, he was silent and uneasy.

'Did you know she'd left the Order?' I said.

'Sure I did.'

'You never told me.'

'Didn't I? Oh it's not important.'

We stood facing one another across a battlefield of empty cups and glasses and dusty records.

Suddenly he slumped into the armchair. His armchair. He spoke quietly as though he were talking to himself, so quietly I had to strain to hear it.

'Actually she didn't exactly leave of her own free will. She didn't have much choice. Her Mother Superior supported the rebels. Dorothy couldn't see eye to eye with her, so she parted company with them, and went to work as a kind of social worker, I suppose you'd call her, among the mountain people.'

'Was that what you were talking about outside? In the garage? I thought you spent a lot of time looking for a few old records.'

'Yeh,' he said. 'Later, she was was captured by the Contras. Dorothy that is.'

He was almost whispering at this time.

'They didn't exactly act like gentlemen. Jesus, when I think of what those bastards did to her ...'

Then he broke down and wept. He hadn't done that in donkey's years. He just wept and wept. I held him. I didn't know what to say. I didn't know what to do. I didn't really know why he was crying.

I held him tight. I felt I was losing him. Perhaps had already lost him. But to what?

After a while, he stopped.

'I'm sorry,' he said. 'It just seemed such a futile gesture.'

'What?' My voice had a croak in it.

'The bloody coffee. The Nicaraguan coffee.'

I didn't know what he was talking about. The coffee had tasted fine. Good in fact. Not as good as our normal, but that could be a matter of taste.

'Just like my whole bloody life,' he went on. 'Gestures, that's all. Singing the songs, subscribing to the right causes, buying Nicaraguan coffee. Gestures. She went out, put her life on the line. And paid the price.'

He wept. A lot.

I wept too. Tears of gratitude. I hadn't lost him. I'd just misunderstood the whole thing. Misread the picture.

Problems and challenges are the same. It's how you look at them that counts.

Allegiance

Maura Treacy

Once before, when she was a child growing up in Woods-gift, another gunman had come to her house ...

It was early one morning at the beginning of winter. Sara awoke to hear her father leaving for work; the wheels crunched the gravel as he led out the pony and cart. Some days he walked to work, but this was Saturday and the Brigadier was to give him timber to bring home for the shed he was building. The Saturday before that there was a barrel of apples and, the week before that again, a bed was sent down from the House for Sara; her bed was passed on to Jamie, leaving the cot for the baby.

Her father came back to shut the gate and she heard his subdued voice as he urged the pony onto the road. He hardly spoke these days. Even the night before when the other men sat around the fire talking about the ambush earlier that week in which several soldiers were wounded, and Nicholas Martin said that that was the stuff to give them, her father sat and frowned in silence.

'We'll show them whose country they're in,' Jim Flynn said. And Nicholas agreed but said it shouldn't be left to the few to put up a fight.

'You'll serve no purpose,' her father warned them and, turning to her mother, he asked, 'Are you leaving that child up all night?'

'All right, Sara,' her mother said. 'Off you go.'

Sometime later her mother came upstairs to settle her down for the night and to check that she'd said her prayers. She sprinkled holy water around the bed and made the Sign of the Cross on Sara's forehead.

The men were leaving and her father had gone out to see them safely across the river. They were going home across the fields because now the soldiers were on the roads at night. Sometimes they knocked on the door, demanding to

139

know who was in the house, and late one night they had barged in and searched all the rooms.

'And then you say we're not involved,' her mother cried. 'Nicholas is right.'

'You have no use minding Nicholas, or any of these,' her father said. 'Making big fellows of themselves.'

Now Sara lay in bed waiting for her mother to call her. Daylight spread dismally over the white walls of the room; on the windowsill a jugful of flowers, first their shape then gradually a hint of their colours, emerged and on her bed the brightest red squares of the plaid rug surfaced from the darkness.

It had rained again during the night and now that it had stopped there were odd creaking and snapping noises in the roof. Water still trickled from the chute into the barrel at the corner of the house. The sound of the pony and cart dwindled away beyond the hill; it was still there, however faintly, and the next moment it was gone altogether. She used to panic then as if her father couldn't exist any more because she couldn't see or hear him and she would run downstairs. But her mother preferred her to wait until she was called, when she was ready to give her her breakfast.

Later in the morning she would kneel on a chair at the table to watch as her mother peeled potatoes while on the hob the brisket was simmering with an onion or two bobbing and rolling in the water; and when her mother went over to put more coal on the fire, Sara would take a few shells of peas or slices of carrot or turnip and go outside to eat them. Sitting on the stile of the well-field she'd watch the road for her father.

When she saw him in the distance she'd run to meet him and on the way home she'd tell him everything that had happened during the morning or if anyone had called in. During the dinner her mother would tell him how she had spent the morning and he'd listen again, trying not to smile when sometimes she used the very same words he'd already heard from Sara. Before he went back he'd stand in the doorway as if looking around for signs of danger.

'You'll be all right there now, till I get home? Don't

answer the door to anyone you don't know. Don't be foolish now.'

Her mother would tell him to go along now or he'd be late; nobody had bothered them in a long time, but if it made him happy, she said, she'd lock the door after he'd gone. But she never did.

Now Sara could hear her working in the kitchen below. She heard her open the door and then come back for the pot of potatoes and corn she'd been heating up for the hens.

The house was very still then and Sara was drifting into a daydream when she was startled by footsteps on the gravel below. After a pause someone knocked on the door. She sat up: lying down she could hear nothing but the pounding of her own heart. The knock came again. There was something odd about it, almost as if the caller half-hoped not to be heard.

Sara slipped out of bed and tiptoed to the window. She looked up and down the road but in the grey, damp, early morning there was nothing, no army lorry or anything else, to be seen.

The caller moved away, around by the side of the house, keeping close to the wall so that from her window Sara could see nothing. Then she heard her mother's voice and in a moment she and the caller came into the kitchen, stopping outside the door first to scrape their shoes.

Sara pulled her pinafore on over her nightdress. Jamie was still asleep and the baby had been carried downstairs when her parents were getting up. Quietly, cupping the knob between both hands, she opened the door. She crossed the landing to the top of the stairs and slowly, her back rubbing against the wall, she edged down a few steps until she could see into the kitchen.

On the table the oil-lamp was burning low and her mother, in crossing back and forth between fire, dresser and table, cast a shadow on the wall by the stairs. She had cut strips of bacon and was spreading them on the hot pan. The kettle was boiling on the hob and when the bacon began to fry she cut some bread and set the table.

As she worked she talked and as he was about to answer

141

the man stopped, turned his head and looked up the stairs to where Sara stood transfixed. His watchful expression relaxed. Her mother looked up to see what had alerted him.

'It's all right. Come on down, Sara,' she said and went on talking. 'We get off light enough, I suppose, around here,' she was saying, 'compared to some. Still, you'd ask yourself what right have they to encroach on people at all in their own homes.'

She cracked another egg on the edge of the pan.

Sara came slowly down the remainder of the stairs, keeping the strange man in sight all the time. His coat was drying out on the back of a chair in front of the fire, wisps of steam rising from the heavy cloth.

'I'll get your own breakfast for you, by-and-by,' her mother explained to Sara as she slid the fried eggs on to the plate of rashers and set it on the table before the stranger. 'There now, get that inside you.'

He was slumped at the table, his head propped between his hands: in the quiet and warmth of the kitchen, he was almost asleep.

'God, ma'am, I never meant you to go to all that trouble.'

'It's no trouble,' she said grimly. She still had the pan of hot fat in her hands. 'Tell me, would you eat a bit of fried bread if I put it on for you?'

For a moment it seemed as if he hadn't heard. Then he began to smile.

'Fried bread! Jesus, ma'am, there's nothing I'd like better,' he said and slowly straightened up, blessed himself and began to eat.

She rearranged his wet coat over the chair. Then she filled a bowl of porridge for Sara.

'How do you manage for something to eat, or a place to sleep?' she asked him.

'The people are very good to us, ma'am, as a rule,' he said.

And later that morning, when he had rested for an hour by the fire, the stranger put on his dry coat and boots and a fresh pair of socks her mother had found for him.

Sara and her mother stood at the door for a while, tense

142

and shivering in the swollen stillness of a morning after rain and, when there was no sight or sound of anybody on the road, her mother signalled to him to come out.

And he went away then, down through the fields behind their house, keeping close to the hedges until he reached the shelter of the woods.

But even as he stood at the corner of the house to look and listen while her mother watched the road, Sara saw huge drops of rainwater from the eaves splashing onto his shoulders and already soaking into his coat again which had taken so long to dry. In his pocket he now had a small parcel of food her mother had wrapped up for him. Inside his coat he carried a gun.

Soon afterwards Nicholas Martin called with the post.

'What do you think, Nicholas?' her mother greeted him. 'Do we stand in danger of the river flooding again with all this rain?'

At dinnertime her father was near the gate before she went out to meet him.

'I thought you were letting me down,' he said. 'But there, gate open and all for me. You're a topping girl.'

'It's as well not to say anything at all to your father, it would only upset him,' her mother had suggested. 'You know now what he's like for worrying.'

So instead Sara told him what Nicholas had said about the river and the danger of flooding.

But years later, when the Troubles were over, her mother would often recall that morning and wonder again what had become of the man on the run, and to the end of her life she had cherished the memory of her own part in the fight for Irish freedom and she would tell the story over and over again to Sara's children.

And Sara, in turn, told her own grandchildren.

But that was a lifetime ago.

Now it was morning again, in her daughter's house where, shortly before daylight, Sara had prepared breakfast for the three armed men who had held the family at gun-

143

point throughout the night.

Soon afterwards they got ready to leave. She listened for the unsticking of the tarmac from under the tyres as the family car glided down the slope to the gate. Her daughter was driving, with one of the armed men beside her, and another, in the back seat, giving directions.

The car stopped at the gate before nosing out onto the road where it merged with the morning traffic speeding towards the city.

The children screamed in terror after their mother, and terror for their father still tied up and gagged in a corner of the room, and terror of the third gunman who had stayed behind with them.

Sara tried to calm the children, to reassure them even now that nothing terrible was going to happen: these were their own countrymen, so how could they have anything to fear from them?

But the children did not believe her now, and again her grandson asked, 'Why did you let them in?'

An International Incident

Emma Cooke

It is late afternoon in Southern Turkey and I'm sitting on the beach. The deckchair is a faded blue and I'm wearing the pink canvas shoes I bought on last year's holiday in Lanzarote. Lanzarote with its ancient history, its heather coloured mountains, and its volcanoes – some of which spout steam hot enough to cook a steak. What else can I say about Lanzarote except that it's the place where we met the Martins.

The sand here is pebbly. I can't remember much about the sand in Lanzarote. There we spent most of our time beside the pool cultivating our friendship with the Martins. We met on the 'plane from Ireland and hit it off immediately. It seemed that we had all visited the same places. We had even, amazingly, celebrated our wedding anniversaries in the same deluxe restaurant in a Florentine alleyway. It was incredible that it had taken us all this time to actually encounter each other. 'Wedding anniversary,' the Martins said in Lanzarote. Now I know they are only living together, biding their time.

Those happy Lanzarote poolside afternoons vanished in a sparkle of delight. I have photographs -- always of the three of us because the fourth one is holding the camera. I'm wearing my blue swimsuit and I'm laughing so hard my stomach bulges, but I obviously don't care. Naturally Anne Martin is as svelte as a Siamese cat. My Eddie and Frank Martin have their arms about each other's shoulders like the Riviera playboys of long ago.

Right now the sun umbrella beside my chair is furled but I'm too apathetic to open it even though I can feel the sun prickling my shoulders. It's a shame that God gave me skin which blisters and freckles. Anne Martin can lie under its brilliant glare for hours and end up looking like burnished bronze. And she can gorge herself on eclairs and ice cream and know she'll never run to fat. (I've already put on half a stone on this trip.)

The afternoon sun is high in the heavens. In Lanzarote evening came quickly. A sudden blackness and then colour-ed lights – and charcoal steaks and red wine. This was fol-lowed by mountainous puddings. Then we had the Chinese man playing one of those music-centre outfits which made him sound like a full orchestra -- while Eddie danced the tango with Anne Martin.

I must concentrate on the soft roar of the surf. Let it fall gently against my ears, soothing me, calming me down. It's much better to sit, letting it all fall away, dissolve, recede. I fix my gaze on the turquoise sea, the shimmering dancing spray.

If I turn my head to the right I can see all the new buildings stretching between here and the town centre. They are moon buildings: buildings which spring up overnight. Since we arrived at this hotel five days ago a new block has been constructed. Yesterday lorries came. One of them car-ried a complete oasis full of palm trees. Another one dis-gorged a special vine-covered trellis to screen off the new swimming pool which had been a muddy hole in the ground the day before. Such instant scenarios make me nervous. I believe in slow solid development and lasting values. Eddie and I have been married for fifteen years.

This morning, as we strolled around the harbour with the Martins, Frank casually mentioned that his and Anne's relationship had never been legalised. They weren't properly married at all. That's one of the reasons I'm lying here in a deckchair feeling emotionally exhausted. He shouted the information over the racket being made by machinery, honking car horns, and the men at work. I seemed to be the only one who got the gist of what he said. My breath was taken away. I couldn't make out why he had chosen this moment to tell us. But he did – while in every direction the new pleasure resort shot up and Anne stood holding her head a little to one side and smiling the way she does when she tangos. It's not that I'm a prude. I don't give a damn what people do with their lives. But the Martins – when we first met them they seemed our perfect counterparts.

When we got back to the hotel another pool and a children's playground had appeared right in front of the block where the four of us have our rooms. Eddie and I have no children because of the difficulties with my first pregnancy. 'So that's why you have no children – it's because you're not actually married,' I said softly to Anne without thinking. It was one of the things we had never got around to discussing in Lanzarote.

She did not look at me directly. I don't think she has looked me squarely in the face once this trip. Instead she stared at the swings and seesaws with a grin as sharp as a hairpin bend. There! I thought, wishing Eddie could see that ugly expression. Then she surprised me by linking my arm in hers and leading me away. As we waited for the men in the patio bar she seemed preoccupied. She knotted a frayed thread and spoke: 'No, Molly, you're quite wrong,' she said. 'Frank and I just couldn't bear to bring a child into a world which is going to destroy itself by nuclear war.'

My first reaction was to laugh, and then to jeer. Then I wanted to make her look at me while I told her of my own experience – of the pain, the blood, the subtle disapproving comments of my mother-in-law when she found that she would never have a grandchild. And of how good Eddie had been about it, how very good. I wanted to ask her what the hell she meant by having designs on Eddie but I kept quiet.

This afternoon she and Frank and Eddie have gone up to town together. That has been the pattern on this trip. The three of them versus myself. Towards the end in Lanzarote I realised that we should never have made space for the Martins in our lives but I was too shocked to protest. I had gone up to our room in the middle of the day and almost walked in on top of her and Eddie making love. I wanted to rush in and drag the silly cow away from my husband and scratch her eyes out but I was unable to speak. I closed the door unnoticed but I kept seeing her jewelled fingers pulling Eddie towards her.

It has been a long year and some of it has been rough going. Eddie has been away from home a good deal. I guess that he has been with Anne five or six times. I have become adept at finding clues: a receipt for a Dublin restaurant, the way he flinches when I reach out towards him in the middle of the night, the amount of whiskey he drinks when we're alone for an evening.

Now I reach for the bottled water beside my chair. It is almost lukewarm, even so, it helps to keep the head clear and the stomach in order. Eddie has been drinking raki steadily since we arrived. Frank doesn't seem to have noticed but Anne has. She keeps darting little glances at him. Not the amused secretive glances of Lanzarote, but little frightened peeps. Meanwhile, I return Frank's smiles and hitch my skirt a little higher under the table as he inches his foot up my leg.

Yesterday, as we looked at the embroidered wedding garments in the museum next door he stood close to me and rested his hand on my bum. 'Gorgeous – I love fat girls,' he whispered. And I took a deep breath to stop myself from screaming at him to remove his filthy paw. The only person I've ever cared about in that way is Eddie. When we got back from Lanzarote I worked hard at making myself forgive him for his infidelity.

'What's wrong, Molly?' he asked at first when I was listless and didn't want to go any place. 'Would you like to see a doctor – or somebody?' He made this suggestion when I went through a phase of feeling that the house was being watched.

'You know I have to go to Dublin every so often,' he said, 'it's company policy.'

'I suppose you'd visit a brothel if it was company policy,' I said one day.

He horrified me by burying his face in his hands and starting to weep. After that I threw no obstacles in his way. When he arrived home saying that Frank Martin had been in touch with him to see if we'd team up for a trip to Turkey I merely shrugged and said, 'you know you've never liked foursomes. Maybe we'll hate them when we meet them again.' I stared hard at him as I spoke.

I know how a man looks when he's in love. He used to

look at me like that once. 'I spoke to Anne as well,' he said. 'She has really set her heart on meeting us both – again. Come on Molly. It might do you good.'

Now I hear their voices calling. I watch them approach. They look frightened and they're all shouting at once.

'America!' Anne cries. 'They've bombed Libya. Their 'planes took off from England.' I don't believe her. I saw her naked in my husband's arms.

'Maggie Thatcher gave permission,' says Frank. His nostrils quiver and he pulls at his chin importantly.

'Civilians killed,' says Eddie. 'Ordinary people.'

'Oh my God,' Anne wails and looks tragically at the sky. 'Children. They killed children.' She rests her head on Frank's shoulder and begins to sob.

For some reason we find ourselves in the Martin's bedroom. The four of us huddle round Frank's little transistor. The station crackles and foreign voices break through. Outside there is a continual hubbub.

Anne keeps making political statements. I don't think she knows the least thing about politics but Frank and Eddie act as if she's a Delphic oracle. Meanwhile I have the strangest feeling of being cut loose and floating into space.

This feeling persists as the evening continues. Nobody yet knows who is shooting at whom. 'From now on it's a caravan in Ballybunion for us,' Anne Martin says. The men argue with other guests in the hotel and everybody except myself starts to behave like raving lunatics. A Turkish barman, on discovering that we're Irish, says, 'when you people go back home shoot Maggie Thatcher.'

'Maggie Thatcher no good,' shout Frank and Eddie in unison.

I know who I'd like to shoot.

'Oh, the relief!' Anne cries when somebody arrives to say that the rumour about further hostilities is false and there is no danger of holidaymakers being stranded here indefinitely. She is even able to make tears run down her face, which Frank and Eddie take turns to dab away. I watch in amazement as her mascara begins to run.

Meanwhile, I sit on my wooden seat feeling my heart

turn into a withered prune. It is intensely humid. Ireland is a long, long way away; even further away than Lanzarote. The windows are wide open and there is a tiny crescent moon in the dark sky. In my loose white dress I fell like a gigantic cabbage butterfly. I hear the music starting up and then her voice saying, 'who's going to dance? Oh, I've got to dance.' But I don't turn around. I lean against the sill and concentrate on the noisy frogs who always start their chorus as soon as the night falls.

'Molly ... Molly ... Molly.'

They can call me as much as they like but I'm listening to the frogs. In a while I'll go out and join them. The swamp is just across the road.

Barney, Ellie, Des and the Couple in the Car

Joe O'Donnell

The door hissed shut and Barney jumped back as the bus accelerated. It was the last 42C and it was full. The conductor wouldn't let him on at the stop and Barney had jumped the bus in Store Street hoping to squeeze on unnoticed. It hadn't worked.

The conductor was middle-aged, slightly bald, slightly fat and very tired. He had grabbed a fistful of the thin polyester at the shoulder of Barney's black suit, called him a punk and thrown him off.

Him? A punk! Barney wasn't a punk. He was just Barney: twenty, one of the young people of Ireland beloved of the Pontiff, a social statistic making what was left of his dole stretch to what was left of Saturday night.

He stood in the middle of the road and roared:

'You can stick your bleedin' bus!'

Oh my God! She hadn't aged a minute. There she was, singing 'Donna Donna Donna'; just as she had done twenty years ago. Rings on her fingers, those strong brown capable fingers strumming the guitar. Joan Baez, singing somewhere in the open to a crowd of thousands.

Ellie, mid-thirties slackening to forty caught a snatch of the opening as the kids slalommed through the channels searching for 'something good'. There was the usual row when she insisted on watching Joan Baez. It had ended with them banging out of the room.

Curled on the settee, her legs folded under her, she hugged herself in nostalgic delight. My God, she hadn't done that in ages. Made her feel like a young one again.

And Joan Baez singing away. All the old songs that she and Des had sung ages ago. Had joined in and marched to, learned off and dreamed on, and all but forgotten until now. Sod the kids! Des was on late shift, and here was Joan Baez singing.

> Suzanne takes you down
> To a place by the river ...

Singing for peace. Singing for her.

Cretin! Dog breath! Scabby dipstick!

Barney had worked himself into a right fury by the time he reached the Five Lamps. The injustice of it! The sodding injustice of it! It was going to take him an hour, hour and a half to get to Darndale.

A cafe near the bridge threw a patch of red neon across the empty pavement. Three gulls, like white ghosts, swooped down on the road, settled and picked at something. A wailing ambulance scorched by, its blue light winking and the gulls swept up again, mewling in protest.

Barney pushed open the cafe door and sat down. The room was sour with the fug of rancid grease, and the reek of fish and chips. It made his stomach growl. A dark haired young one was swabbing down the plastic counter-top.

'A one 'n one to eat here,' he said, 'and a glass of milk.'

The waitress went on swabbing.

'We're closed for the night.'

'Could you not manage even just one little single?' Barney asked, toying with the uncapped vinegar bottle and the salt cellar.

'Frying's finished,' the girl said. 'We're closed for the night.'

'But you're still open.'

'We're not serving. I told you we're closed.'

'Well, who's seeing you home?'

'We're closed. I'm tired. Okay?'

'Just gimme a cup of coffee. That won't kill you.'

'The machine's off the boil.'

'Ah buggar the machine. Put it on the boil again.'

'I told you we're closed.'

Barney spilled some vinegar on the table, began to doodle it around with his finger.

The girl looked at him uncertainly for a second, and then went through a red and green plastic curtain behind the counter. Barney heard an agitated staccato of Italian through the curtain. He sauntered across to the juke box and punched out Les Enfants and 'Slip Away'.

I sit alone
Nowhere to go
I sit alone
Unhappy man ...

The door opened, and a small fat man with a moustache came out. His arms were dark and hairy under the blue pin-striped shirt. He stooped down and snapped the plug out of the juke box. The lights went out, and the machine hissed like the bus doors.

'We closed,' said the man.

'Just a bleedin' coffee,' said Barney.

'I said: we closed.'

Barney stood there.

The man yawned, carefully removed his greasy white apron, gave a final flick to the sleeve of his shirt, and then swooped on Barney. Barney felt his left wrist doubled up behind him. The man took him by the scruff of the collar with his other hand, and hustled him out the door.

'Go home. We tired.'

The door slammed. Barney stuck his face against the glass. 'The whole shaggin' country's bleedin' tired,' he shouted. 'What we all need is a month in bed.'

The crowd was singing like a huge choir. There must have been millions of them – well, thousands of them. Tens of thousands. Young faces, old faces. All against violence. All singing along with Joan.

The answer my friend,
Is blowing in the wind.
The answer is

Blowing in the wind.

Joan sang it in English, in French, in German, in Spanish, and in something that could have been Japanese. Ellie sang along too. Once the kids looked in, raised eyes to heaven, skittered. She yelled at them. They scuttled out.

One thing Ellie noticed with a certain bitchy satisfaction. The cameras went behind at one time to show the huge crowd. They also showed a back view of Joan, and Ellie saw that Joan's backside had spread more than a little since the 1960s. Just as Ellie's had, 'though maybe not as much.

It was a long programme. There was even a chance that Des would see a bit of the end. He would have enjoyed it. 'Though maybe not. Recently when things came on about the 1960s or about the Beatles or hippies or things like that, he seemed to get cross and wanted to change channels.

Then those flats just before Newcomen Bridge: that was where the Germans had bombed the houses during the war. It was his Da's First Communion day. His da was only seven and *his* Da – Barney's grandad – had taken him on that May morning to see the devastation.

As a treat.

And told him about this man who had looked out of the window to see what the noise was and got his head sliced off by a pane of flying glass. Clean off! Whoosh! Just like your man, the scientist bloke in *The Omen*. That's why the place always gave him the creeps. Always thought he'd see a man, a *headless* man, looking out of the window.

Bloody stupid really. I mean how could a *headless* man look out of a window? What would he be looking *with*, much less looking *at*?

That straightened out, he set off whistling in a better mood. Near the Bingo Hall that his Da remembered as the Strand Cinema, Barney stood in front of a cigarette machine. He pulled the drawer a few times to see if there was any change in the machine. Then he thumped the side.

He was about to kick it when out of the corner of his eye, he saw the blue Ford Sierra pulling into the curb. Two big

154

guys got out. Barney needed no telling. Plain clothes. Oh Jaysus, here we go again!

Best get in first.

'Bloody machine has just swallowed me last few bob!' Barney shook his head in mock despair.

They didn't answer.

Keep the head, Barney. No smart answers. Be polite, but not unnaturally so. Answer all questions truthfully.

Well, as truthfully as the situation demands. Otherwise trouble.

He was polite. He answered the questions – name, address, where he was coming from, where he was going. Showed them the certificate (name, and address authenticated) of the ANCO course he had just finished.

Tried a joke: 'I'm a government artist. Yeh, I draw the dole. Hah-hah.'

It died.

While one of them was asking the questions, the other put some 50p pieces into the machine and got a packet of Rothmans.

'Don't seem much wrong with that machine, son.'

'Story of my life. I'm just unlucky,' said Barney.

'No, son, consider yourself *lucky*. Move on.'

Barney smiled. Good natured. Man to man. Then: 'I suppose a lift's out of the question?'

The big one opened his packet of Rothmans. He took out two. Stuck one in Barney's mouth, and put the other carefully in the top pocket of Barney's jacket. Patted it firmly.

'Don't push your luck, son. Two fags should see you home, so there won't be any more need to – ah – interfere with private property.'

A cold thin thread of sweat coursed down his spine with relief.

The tears were coursing down Ellie's face; Joan was singing the Bob Dylan song, 'It's All Over Now, Baby Blue'.

Oh my God, if the kids came in now and caught her like this. Or Des. He'd call her all the eegits from sea to sun. He'd understand. But he'd pretend not to.

Then Joan sang some new songs. Songs about Vietnam and Chile and El Salvador and Argentina. And people disappearing. And they showed pictures of mothers, long lines of them outside somewhere official, carrying photos of their sons and daughters who had simply vanished. Just gone out one night and never came home.

He crossed the road near the Protestant chapel and walked on down over the Tolka Bridge. Here Brian Boru had beaten the crap out of the Danes or was it the other way around? History was never Barney's strong point.

It was low tide and the river smelled bad. At the traffic lights on Fairview corner, a small car drew up alongside him and a woman's voice asked: 'Are you going far? Would you like a lift?'

Barney said he was slogging it to Darndale and the man who was driving told him to hop in.

The man had a briar pipe in his mouth which burbled every time he drew on it.

'We're going to Howth,' the man said without taking the pipe out of his mouth, 'we can drop you on the way.'

Barney thanked them and awkwardly climbed over the front seat as the woman got out to let him in.

They had a son about Barney's age, they said. He had left home three years ago, and they hadn't had sight nor light of him since. They always gave a lift to boys of Barney's age late at night. They were never quite sure why.

She called him Freddy. He called her 'mother'.

The woman had a crumpled newspaper and kept reading out bits to her husband who just said 'uh-uh' from time to time.

'Listen to this Freddy,' she'd say and they'd chuckle over this and that. Barney settled down in the back seat wreathed in chuckles and tobacco smoke.

The credits were rolling after the Joan Baez programme. It had finished with the crowd lighting matches and cigarette

156

lighters in the dark. The orange flames had thrown gaunt shadows onto the happy faces lending them a type of grotesque horror.

The concert, she read, was recorded on Bastille Day. Ellie knew that Bastille Day was some sort of French holiday, but for the life of her couldn't remember what the Bastille was. It annoyed her. The kids were in bed, so she couldn't ask them. And Des wasn't home yet. He was on 'lates' tonight. She hoped he was all right. He'd been having a lot of trouble with yobbos on the late buses recently.

The lady read out a statement from the IRA claiming responsibility for the death of an electrician in Lisburn.

'Strange word to use, wouldn't you say, Freddy?'

'What word's that, mother?'

'Responsibility.'

The man burbled his pipe. 'See what you mean,' he chuckled, 'damn strange.'

'Des?' she said as soon as he'd put his head inside the door. 'Des, what was the Bastille?'

'Sort of prison in Paris, love. Used for politicals. It was torn down during an argy-bargy in seventeen-eighty-something.'

That was her Des. Head of knowledge.

'Your eyes are red. Have you been crying again?'

The lady turned to look at Barney. She smiled. He was sleeping. Peacefully.

And The Street Went Blind

Pat Boran

Labourers don't spit for the same reasons as the rest of us. Granted theirs is thirsty work, work which demands the regular clearing of the mouth and throat; but their spitting is also a salutation, an ice-breaker, a ritual of friendship. I tried to remind myself of this as they spat upon my arrival by taxi, spat upon my approach across the hazardous stew of mud and stones which comprised the site, spat as one of the younger ones forced his last cigarette on me. We puffed in silence, wondering what to make of each other. An old woman and her dog linked past where we stood in the sun, surrounded by the half-demolished buildings of an area which my memory insisted was home.

'Ten minutes,' said a tall one whom I presumed to be the foreman. He spat uncomfortably. 'It's just that we've got our orders.' And he walked over to where the others had gathered for a tea-break, absently tapping a spoon which he'd produced from his pocket against the side of his leg.

'C'mon,' they were shouting, impatiently, while one or two had already sugared and stirred with the handles of screwdrivers or whatever.

The foreman turned: 'Ten minutes, mind.'

'Spoon, spoon, spoon,' they chorused, banging their tin cups on the oil-drum table.

It had been my father's place – an optician's, if you could call it that – in the beginning, anyway. Pieces of broken spectacles lay in the dust of the big window which was shaped like an eye. At one time the whole city recognised it, commented on its aptness, would discuss the peculiar feeling of finding one's own reflection in the glass, as if the city were constantly watching.

We'd started out a long time before, selling spectacles – OK, we'll call them glasses – which we kept in a shoe box on the counter of our general store. The glass was already in them when you arrived. You simply selected the ones you felt you could see best with from the range. If one of the lenses was damaged (as was often the case), or just unsuitable, my father would switch it with one from another pair. No problem. Frames with both lenses damaged he gave to an army of old beggars patrolling the inner-city streets, who seemed delighted to stumble about, crashing over dustbins. In the beginning he'd simply removed the useless lenses and given them the unwanted empty frames, but they'd felt deceived and were, in any case, happier to suffer what they obviously felt to be 'strong medicine'.

My job, charging in from school with a mouthful of sherbet, was to keep the precious lenses clean and, if possible, intact after their often severe handling. There was also the important duty of keeping all convex lenses out of direct sunlight in case we should all be burned in our beds. How my dad thought the sun might shine so brilliantly at night, I never questioned. Not that it mattered: I never fully understood the difference between concave and convex anyway, and arbitrarily divided the lenses into those I liked the shape of and those I didn't. And, needless to say, the place never burned down.

Eventually my father had a young girl come in, and the presentation and care of the glasses, entrusted to her, became more elaborate, even baffling. She produced rolls of a material which she called chamois, but which wasn't to be found in any dictionary I examined. We used it to wrap the glasses for protection – a move which I felt was not gentle to the sensitivities of our customers. Heavy or dirty objects were forbidden in the area used for preparing new frames, and she had the walls decorated with black and white pictures of girls wearing ornate and ugly 'high-fangled specs' which she claimed were all the rage. And she even stayed late once in a while to touch up the pictures with crayon so they looked all modern and special.

But the task of cleaning the lenses, the delicate things now kept under the counter – that important task remained mine.

By this time many people began to insist on some form of examination before parting with their money, so my dad asked around and eventually came up with one of those letter charts – big letters on top, small letters subordinate. It was the only parable he used.

After a time he got to enjoy his endless pacing back and forth in front of that chart (sometimes with a pointer in his hand!), tut-tutting at each error or hesitation, which was, of course, designed to throw the customer-stroke-patient into a wild panic where only the best glasses would suffice. Though, of course, he was too kind a man and too generous with his sympathies to allow an ageing neighbour to depart distraught.

'A cup of hot tea. The only cure.'

Nevertheless, the shoe box of old reliables remained under the counter for those older members of society who preferred to trust their own judgement in the matter of selection, and leave scientific advances to the next generation. Perhaps it wasn't possible to see the Dublin they knew through modern lenses ...

Standing before the window, I watched the reflection of the labourers grouped around their stove as if it were the middle of winter. In the corner of the window I could see the wrecking ball, the bulldozers, the trucks waiting to carry the rubble away. But, more importantly, I felt the window was watching all this, too. I felt the desire to go inside and look out, to see the world again from its perspective.

By the time my father passed on, the area was already in decline and, though the two events were in most ways unconnected, they seemed together to herald the end of an era. Slowly things vanished; neighbours moved off; the bus-stops in the street were rearranged to make way for the expected increase in traffic. Old buildings came down in clouds of dust; sometimes new, concrete things went up in their places, sometimes nothing – empty spaces guarded by hoardings, splattered with rock concert posters or pictures of smiling politicians, their lips touched up to tantalise babies.

The eye looked out on a town disfigured, a city with its teeth kicked in.

'Four o'clock,' said the foreman.

I used to get home from school about now, dash across the street into the doorway, tidy my hair, chuck my satchel into the cupboard and begin polishing glasses, polish until tea-time.

Carefully I put my hand on the door handle. It felt strange reaching down to it. The door opened like the lid of an old school desk. I went in, closing it behind me, shutting the present outside. The floorboards had rotted. I could taste sherbet on my lips. My father's three-legged stool lay on its broken back. Jewels of spectacle glass winked in the dusty spotlights of boarded side windows. Under the counter I found the shoe box, exactly where it had always been, now full of skeletal remains and broken glass, the epitaph 'spectacles' on the side in my father's clumsy script, faded by years – my years away from Dublin, of not stopping long enough to remember.

I had forgotten the pictures of the ladies which could stand unsupported on the counter. Perhaps they'd been put there during my father's period of illness when the business had started to fall apart unsupervised.

A car pulled up outside and I went to the window.

The youngest labourer was pointing to his watch.

'Four o'clock,' he mouthed.

Someone who appeared to be important walked over to where the workmen were relaxing. They pointed to the window and dug their heels into the gravel. The foreman bit his lip. Others of them spat.

I didn't have much time.

Down in the bottom of the window I noticed a pair of black-framed glasses, their arms folded almost in waiting. Under a constant drip one lens was clear, the other an opaque grey – a piece of slate. My father would stand at that window, his hands clasped behind his back, bobbing up and down on his toes, so that his head always moved but his tan-coloured shop-coat hung motionless around him. He always had his bifocals (which he didn't need) perched down on the end of a nose which he likened to Agatha Christie stories – 'finely crafted with a sudden twist on the end'. I'd look up at his long face and find his eyebrows magnified into wild bushes while his eyes appeared like tiny green peas. Sometimes he'd jab a hand into my hair, point to the shoe box, and I'd slouch over to the counter, pretending to be his prisoner. He'd stamp his heels like an angry captor, and then, if someone came in, look totally confused as he tried to remember how opticians should behave. I'd drag my feet, trying to make him laugh as he magnified people's eyes so that they looked like giant insects in his dark laboratory.

I took the glasses from the window, and wiped the grey lens on my sleeve until, still semi-clouded, the world appeared like a daguerreotype, the edges of vision fading to a blur. The men were still talking, some of them smoking, the new arrival with his hands folded high across his chest. Like the glasses. Behind them was a tower of as-yet empty offices whose mirrored windows reflected the chaos of the street, threw back the image in rejection. The reflections made the new building almost invisible in the wilderness of rafters and rubble.

The top of the shop counter was made of a substance I used to call 'Moonstone'. It seemed to be formed by green crystals, like slabs of coloured ice, except that it was not particularly cold to touch. Around the edge was a band of metal which held the Moonstone in place. The corners of it were buckled into little lips on which we often snagged our clothes, and sometimes our fingers.

I lightly made a fingerprint in the dust. It looked as though the finger had been there for years, and was being lifted only now to reveal this tiny green island in an ancient sea. And in a way it had been there all those years, and I wasn't so much revisiting as leaving for the first time.

I opened the door.

A football sped down the street, bouncing along the footpath with me in pursuit, so that sometimes I went left and it went right, the two of us like characters from the musical *Oliver*, dashing through the schoolchildren, past the coloured shop-fronts, the polished brass of hall doors, women pushing prams, girls skipping, someone sweeping the footpath outside his house, old Abraham collecting scrap metal in his little pram, until, with some fancy footwork, I trapped it and brought it back to our game at the other end of the street where a cigarette break had been called in my absence.

Standing there in the doorway, I saw myself as a boy with a ball dash past ...

The daylight dazzled me a little. The workmen were already standing by their machines like racing drivers. One or two even had coloured hard-hats on. A group of young children tossed stones about in idle expectation.

An ice-cream van jingled by, heading for new suburbs.

They watched it go.

And a woman pointed, holding her toddler by the hand as he strained to reach a muddy puddle with his lollipop.

The machines moved, inched forward, gravel whizzing from their tracks in all directions, ringing off the stacks of scrap-metal fittings and corrugated iron – 'luvly bits of metal' old Abraham would drag away to his little flat off South Circular Road – if he were still around.

I shut the door behind me, walked past the schoolkids who thought they were seeing a ghost appear from the condemned building.

The labourers stood about, spitting and nodding to one another through the dust, as they have stood and spat since time began.

The taxi I had come in was still parked in the same spot, the driver stripped to his string vest, leaning against the bonnet of his old Anglia and licking an ice-cream which, through no provocation of mine, he explained he had bought when an ice-cream van had to stop to avoid a chicken.

'No, no, honest to Jaysus, a chicken. Strolling across the road.'

I sat in to his car. With a gulp he finished his ice-cream.

In the wing mirror everything looked small. It was like sitting there watching television, that same feeling of distance. The engine started somewhere behind us. I turned to see the big ball take aim, swing back and punch its first great hole in the walls. Rafters groaned, glass shattered; the big eye-window tumbled in on itself. The building squinted, briefly. And the street went blind.

The Clear Night of Day

Michael Coady

Two in the morning, the house in silence, and the tree bleeding. Lucy upstairs, her dreaming face a girl's; the children warm and tousled in their bunks.

Snap of the light-switch in the kitchen, the flicker of cold fluorescence showing him hard lines, clean surfaces ready for morning, intimating other days and mornings yet to come, their mundane bread of living waiting to be broken. Hum of the freezer in the silence. The salmon of last September hard and frosted, the process of change arrested in cuts of beef and lamb, food for the table of their lives. And the tree outside, passively bleeding in the darkness.

He sat in dressing-gown and slippers, poured cold milk into a cup. He had eased away from Lucy's warmth, left her sleeping. Left her under cover of that utter innocence which stills the world, draws every eyelid down into the night's oblivion. Down at the stone bridge, unseen, a tide was ebbing and flooding or poised between. Earlier that evening his children had discovered an old Beatles' record. The words reheard in twenty years' perspective. *There's nothing you can do that can't be done.* The brash beat and the song which pulsed its moment. *There's nothing you can sing that can't be sung.* And the bullet waiting to be moulded, formed, sent out to find John Lennon. *Nowhere you can be that isn't where you're meant to be.*

Blindly, we voice our own prophecies.

Cigarette, but no matches. He stretched to the cooker, waited for the metal ring to redden, touched, drew smoke into his lungs. The oak that he had planted would simply live or die without reference to him. Eight years of his tending, his solicitude. He had chosen the place, dug the planting-pit, sledged into it a supporting stake of larch, carefully laid out the roots of the transplanted oak, piled and pressed clay firmly about them. He had bound the tree windfirm to the stake, stepped back and looked on it with a profound satisfaction.

You did not make this tree, but you're a catalyst, an intermediary. You've intervened: you've moved to modify a future landscape. Roots will insinuate themselves into this particular earth; sap will flow, buds swell and break. Branches will leaf and spread themselves to air, to sun and rain. The bole will thicken. Birds will find it as it grows above your stature. You did not make this tree, but put it in this place, arranged a conscious coupling here between particular earth and sky.

Eight years of this tending. Looking up into March branches for confirmation of sapflow into twig and bud. Listening in worry and in darkness when wind buffeted and whined about the house. Buckets of water to sustain it in dry summers. A magical chance glimpse of a blackbird on a branch one early morning.

But who commands the branch and fork of consequence? We appropriate the use of things within our space and time, our chance arrivals and departures, our encounters. The world a web of arrogant appropriation: his, hers, ours, yours, theirs. There's no clear title. We are nomads in a process of continuum. This milk into my mouth. This smoke into my lungs. These bones into the ground.

But yet the tree out there contained, possessed, some given part of him. And so he'd grieved, going out after tea, to find its bark hacked deeply and irreparably, the sapflow broken, perhaps mortally. He had raged helplessly, with an inner violence as dark as that which moved the hand which mutilated. The oak felt nothing; neither resignation nor pain nor rage. It would simply live or die in perfect balance of inexorable force and consequence. Leaves would shrivel, wood turn dry and brittle. Or else the tree would struggle through, its brute scar tangled in its history, knotted darkly in the grain of time. The anger and the bleeding were all his.

In the cold fluorescent light he guessed something of the rage and impotence of a man who watches a child hover between life and death. Beyond the humpy field that used to be the Workhouse graveyard the mail train rattled by in darkness. Bound sacks of envelopes in transit. Cyphered

166

words from heart to living heart, from mind to mind. Sealed privacies and public declarations. Grief and love and friendship, kinship and commerce, touching and distancing.

That strange lost day beside the Bay of Fundy kept returning. The town, its name forgotten, where he had waited four hours for a bus to take him to the U.S. border. A chill rain falling by a quayside high enough to hold the biggest tide-swell in the world. Before he came that day the harbour had emptied, as if the sea had been sucked back into some vast abyss, leaving grounded trawlers thirty feet below the quay like crippled carcasses abandoned by the element which gave them form and function.

The girl on the bus which had brought him to that town. A girl alone and crying. A plain face, nameless to his knowing, her eyes inflamed with weeping. He, a foreigner, had watched her through a two hour journey while he agonised in indecision. What was her name? The cause of her unclothed grief? He knew he should have moved to sit beside her, risk rebuff, embarrassment. That's why it kept returning like a guilt. He should have left his seat and talked to her, stranger to stranger, offering the common currency of human comfort, risking the violation of private space.

Everywhere this maze of misses and of meetings, of lost encounters and random destinations. He'd never know her name or why she wept. A plain girl on a bus in a foreign country, a girl he might have comforted.

That chill wet day, walking the streets of a Canadian town while he waited for the evening bus, he'd felt both lost and strangely liberated. Anonymous for those few hours, he might have been anyone, or no one. The woman in the bank who changed his traveller's cheques hardly raised her eyes, asked for no identification. There are people here, as everywhere, he thought, that I could come to know. There are lives that I could touch, that could touch mine, but never will. He had walked the wet streets, gone into bookshops, a restaurant. Money in his pocket, addresses, a passport with a name, a photograph, a place of origin – but for one afternoon he was without identity, without direction or a history.

Some instinctive impulse from his culture had made him

search the streets for a Catholic church, to sit in its familiar gloom and silence, light a votive candle. But all he chanced upon were plain evangelical churches, their doors locked and barred. He'd bought a newspaper, saw, headlined, the death of Henry Fonda, dropped it into a litter bin and walked on in the rain. In a grimy side-street he heard a man and woman shrill in argument below a basement grating, the man shouting hoarsely – *so why should I give a goddamn if Henry Fonda's dead?*

One day, one place in passing, and a weeping girl he might have comforted.

Everywhere this enigma of encounter. The hour-glass in whose neck we live, the mundane flux of *now* in which we face not towards the future, but downstream towards the past, our only glimpsed reality. Blindly we row against time's current with our backs to the future which swirls and funnels towards us.

Quite suddenly, in his mid thirties, this mystery assailed him from all sides, as if beneath the ordinary, the physical, unsuspected mine-shafts of enigma suddenly opened. This still bowl of oranges at his elbow, the salmon ice-locked in the freezer, his people lying in the earth across the river, Lucy and the children in the innocence of sleep above his head, the tree passively bleeding out there in the darkness and a nameless girl weeping on a bus three thousand miles of ocean and two years ago – all things affirming some rich but baffling music of innumerable notes and chords and voices, never resolving, but finding random, transitory cadences.

There's nothing you can see that isn't shown.

One Sunday morning of snow last February he had gone alone on impulse to the hidden and abandoned churchyard off Main Street, pushed the heavy iron gate against the piled and perfect snow and walked through swirling white to stand in awe and ecstasy inside the roofless church. Beneath this snow, dark honeycomb of bedded generations, promiscuous in anarchy of earth.

Out of the unfathomable air above his head the snow was whirling, tumbling through unroofed space to pile immaculate in drifts within the chancel where bread and wine were reverenced through centuries.

What did they know which moved them to come here, that shadowy procession of generation upon generation?

This place implied innumerable instances, moments, days and lives, mornings and evenings, each as real and integral in its time as every whirling flake of snow about his face. Headstones leaned and huddled, their graven names effaced, made virginal. The living town, hushed under its white coverlet, stood just beyond the gate through which he'd entered. Here every leaning stone bore witness to eyes which had seen and slept, limbs which had stirred to walk or run, to kneel or dance or couple. The sheeted earth on which he stood was peopled by the human act of love, by nakedness, birth-cry, death-rattle. By blood as warm and carnal as his own.

He had looked toward the churchyard gate, wondered at the footprints leading to his feet and realised in shock and something like rapture that the tracks were his own.

He should be sleeping. He took an orange in his hand, felt its roundness. Last thing in bed each night they kissed lightly, as if in parting, before they turned into the singularity of sleep. *There's nothing you can know that isn't known.* New Year's Eve with friends and befuddled by wine and argument, he had lurched to his feet to make some statement and blurted out the words – *in the clear night of day* – grasped what his tipsy mouth had said and knew his tongue had voiced the mystery with which he was surrounded.

Before he went upstairs he opened the front door and looked out into the darkness. In a few hours grey light would infiltrate the valley; later his children would wake, discovering the bread of the familiar and the new. The sky was overcast and he could scarcely see the outline of the tree. It would simply live or die. Eight years of his tending. A casual malevolence had chosen it to mutilate, acting out some blind necessity. Who commands the branch, the fork, of consequence?

Under his feet the stairs creaked in the silence. The tree would go on bleeding in the darkness while he slept.

A Change in the Weather

Ciarán Ó Cualáin

It was my mother speaking. She was telling my father he should change his suit. They were in the kitchen.

'It looks a bit shabby,' she said. 'Put on your really good suit, why don't you? But hurry up.'

I was sitting on the back door step, trying to unravel a fishing line. The line lay in a pile on the ground and I was winding it around a wooden slat. Beside it, on the ground, was a small tin box with hooks and a penknife in it. I'd found the knife in the shed. It was rusty and blunt. My mother didn't know about it. The tin box was an old Oatfield sweet box that I used to keep stamps in before.

When my father had gone upstairs to change, my mother called me in. She was taking a tray of scones from the oven. She cut a scone in half, buttered both halves, put them on a saucer and handed it to me. I held the saucer, waiting for all the butter to melt.

'We'll be going soon,' she said. 'You're a big boy now and I want you to look after things. Remember everything I told you?'

I remembered what she'd told me earlier that morning. To be sure I was here when Aunt Julia called. To always call Aunt Julia by her proper name. Not to complain at mealtimes. Not on any account to use bad language. If anyone called looking for my father, to say he'd be back in a few days.

'And don't be fighting with your brother,' she said. 'Remember you're older.'

She sat on the couch in the living-room and began to brush her hair. She sorted through things in her handbag. My brother came and stood by the doorway watching. When she was ready she called him over and gave him a kiss.

Then she went out to the car where my father stood waiting with all the doors open because of the heat. They waved and shouted goodbye and we stood at the gate and watched the car until it turned the corner at the end of our road.

My brother stepped onto the first bar of the gate and started to hum to himself. I caught him around the waist and tickled him. He laughed and struggled to get free. I kept on tickling him and he slipped down onto the cement path. He was still laughing. When he stopped laughing he lay there and said, 'I've a pain in my tummy.'

'Softy,' I said.

Later on Aunt Julia came. She wanted to know at what time my parents had gone. She asked if my mother had left any message. Then she went looking for my brother and found him playing with stones, in amongst the trees behind the shed.

When we were all in the kitchen, she said, 'Now, I'm sure you're going to be good boys.' And I said yes and went into the living-room to find a book to read. My brother stayed in the kitchen and Aunt Julia got him to help her wash the potatoes.

While she was getting ready the dinner my Aunt sang 'Che Sara Sara'. Then she tried to teach it to my brother. But my brother wasn't interested. He had his own songs. He sang 'Whiskey on a Sunday'. And then 'Cool Clear Water', which he'd learnt from one of my father's '78s.

'Oh, you only know drinking songs, you scallywag,' my Aunt said.

'They're just songs,' he said.

For dinner we had chops and potatoes and cabbage. It was the same as we usually had except Aunt Julia made a kind of gravy for the meat. The gravy was too salty and I scraped it off the chop, but my brother said 'I don't like this stuff,' and he wouldn't eat any more. Aunt Julia told him to stay at the table until everyone was finished.

My brother said, 'When is Mammy coming back?'

'When she gets the baby,' Aunt Julia said.

After a bit my brother said, 'Where do they get the

babies from?'

'Babies are given by God,' Aunt Julia said.

'Why don't you get God to give you a baby?' my brother said.

I looked at my Aunt. All she said was, 'Look how your brother ate up all his dinner.'

All that evening I sat in the shade and waited for the man called Kicker Kennedy to call to take me fishing. I unwound the rest of the line. Then I dug for worms. After I had twenty I gave up.

When nobody came I went looking for birds' nests in the hedges around the garden. There were hardly ever any and I didn't find one this time.

The next day we were playing football. Aunt Julia came out to the garden.

She said, 'Well boys, you have a new baby sister.'

'What's her name?' said my brother.

'You'll have to wait and see,' she said.

That night Aunt Julia said, 'Say a special prayer for your Mammy. And one for your new sister too.' I wondered what kind of prayer you should say for a baby, but eventually I thought of something.

I had forgotten about fishing when Kicker Kennedy called to the house. I was planning on building a tree-house before my parents came home, and I was looking through a hobby book for instructions, when he knocked on the back door and came in. He didn't see me at first. He spoke to Aunt Julia who was sitting by the range.

'Any news?' he said, and Aunt Julia shook her head. When he saw me he said, 'How's the soldier?' He always called me that.

'What about the fishing?' he said.

When we were leaving Aunt Julia didn't say 'Mind your sandals' or 'Don't get wet'. She sat in the living-room, waiting for something.

Kicker Kennedy lived by the lake. He lived there with his sister, and a boy my father said was his nephew, but the boys in school called him other things.

The first day we went on the lake my father came with us. While we sat with the lines in the water, the Kicker sang songs. Songs I'd heard on the radio, like 'The Black Velvet Band' and 'The Streets of Baltimore' and other songs, like 'A White Sport's Coat and a Pink Carnation' and 'The Yellow Rose of Texas'.

When he didn't know all the words he'd make something up. He'd put on an American accent. 'This is a real hurtin' song,' he'd say and start 'He'll Have to Go'. My father would listen, but he wouldn't sing. He'd look at me and smile.

On this day the Kicker didn't sing. He asked me riddles. 'What's the biggest and most obvious thing in the world and yet nobody can see it?' What was it? I can't remember.

He told me a story. It was a long story about something that happened in America and I soon lost interest. I watched the water and hoped a fish would bite. The lake was flat and empty. Through the haze in the distance I could see small islands with stone walls and bushes. At the end of the story Kicker Kennedy said, 'Just goes to show you. There are some people who have all the luck and some who can never get any.'

We fished all that evening. We caught twenty-five perch and we almost caught a pike. 'The next time,' the Kicker said, 'we'll get one.'

My brother was up at the back of the garden, gathering armfuls of grass and piling it in a heap. He didn't see me. In the coal shed I spread the fish on a newspaper and arranged them according to size. I looked at their damp bodies, their blueness in the dim light.

I went into the house. Aunt Julia was standing by the living-room window, looking out. She knew I was there, but she didn't turn around.

'What's wrong?' I said.

'Sit down on the couch,' she said.

'It's to do with your Mammy,' she said.

What I remember most about the hospital is the whiteness; all the walls glaring in the room where they kept my mother. But she wasn't my mother anymore.

'Your Mammy's gone,' Aunt Julia had said.

Why was she saying these things to me? I looked at my father. I wanted him to say something. Aunt Julia took me outside. She said, 'Be a good boy. Your Daddy needs your help now.'

I was certain then that lots of things were changing.

My sister wasn't brought home until after the funeral. The cot was put in the living-room during the day. She cried a lot. My brother stood at the end of the cot and watched her.

'What's her name?' he said.

But she didn't have a name yet.

Aunt Julia came most days. I'd hear her talking as she worked about the house. She said she couldn't let things go to rack and ruin. She said there was no point in just moping.

I kept out of the house. Mostly I sat on the ground in a cool place amongst the cypress trees and tried to think of things to do. I would hear all the sounds of traffic and of people coming and going on the road outside. Sometimes I fell asleep.

It was evening. We were in the living-room; the three of us sitting at the table. The cot was in the corner. The baby was crying. I wanted to tell my father to pick up the baby and stop her crying. But he was in a bad mood. He was always in a bad mood now. And Aunt Julia was busy in the kitchen. She brought in a dish of potatoes and served dinner. She didn't go near the cot. Maybe she was pretending she couldn't hear the crying. Everybody started to eat.

After a while, Aunt Julia said, 'Isn't it time she was baptised? What are you going to call her?'

My father didn't answer.

'Didn't Helen have a name in mind?' she said.

My father put down his knife and fork. He hit his fist hard against the table. 'Get out,' he shouted. 'Stop fussing

174

around here and go home to your own bloody husband.'

Afterwards, my father sat at the table, the knife and fork and the plate before him. My brother sat on the edge of the couch. For a long time the baby wouldn't stop crying. But it was as if she wasn't there anymore. She was like some found thing, without a name, that everyone had forgotten.

It got darker. Nobody turned on the light. My brother fell asleep. My father stared at the window as if expecting some sign of a change in the weather. But nothing stirred outside.

Then he started to speak in a low voice.

'Damn you,' he said. 'Damn you to hell.'

He said it, over and over, to himself, quietly, in that house, with the night coming in and all of us gathered around in the darkness.

A Ribbon of Rainbow

Eoin Ó Laighin

The path is pot-holed and the pebbled gravel scrunches underfoot. A green beard of grass grows knee-high in the middle and a mangled mesh of fern and bracken fringes the sides. Russet cows chomp and chew cud in the knobbly field of spiky rushes where long ago Granny Mac rode the black pooka. The house was always visible from the road except in summer when a leafy screen hid it from view, and you had to trudge 500 twisty yards beneath rustling branches before you glimpsed the north gable. The whitewash was a tinted blue and you never went in the front door which was for show, but in the back one which wasn't, and so was always open. Rhubarb and blackberries and potatoes and cabbage grew in the garden then. Dandelion, honeysuckle and bramble allsorts grow there now. The cracked back door is propped shut with a chair to keep out unwanted rain and wind. I push it open. Dust flickers in a shaft of sunlight. I blink and look. I am staring into silence cast by the spell of a drowsy decade. Mrs Coyne rattles the range and kindles the glow inside. Paddy snores in the corner and Mom sorts the towels and swimsuits. Someone calls me from the hillside outside; voices from a bygone time zone ...

From behind the grimy net curtain, the sky is a saturated sponge of sun-streaked grey, drooping and dripping rain. I am alone now in the house of childhood ... I am not a child.

God keep this house from sorrow and alarm,
from sickness, sudden death, from evil sin
and harm

– says the prayer on the wall. The cactus on the sill is sapless, and chipped earthenware in blue and pink clutters the dresser, where an hour-glass is standing useless. I tip it upside down, and mustard dust falls in a thin string. Moments of youth mingle and fade away. There is wind and rain on the

176

window pane and the jumbled bumps of the Twelve Bens are shrouded now in funereal grey ...

I can see a graveyard, a gold enamelled coffin and an oblong earthy hollow. The breastplate glints goodbye and dull clay thuds a drumbeat ...

I cannot see twelve ragged crags out there. I cannot see my father and somehow now, I know he is no more.

My bedroom was the first down the corridor. It was painted yellow and had a carpet in patterned brown, but the bedspread was tweedy blue. I slept on the left, so that I could wake and watch the morning dawn across the moors. I remember lonely, squelchy marshes untainted by habitation save the birds of the bog, unspoiled by vegetation save the feathery, furry purple puffs of heather and woolly bog-cotton. Even sheep grazed nearer home amidst the wigwam clumps of burnt umber turf. It's empty now; a bare bed with mothy mattress and a dusty chest of drawers. I lie down. There is no pillow. I stare at the cracked ceiling of Lough Corrib and Lough Mask, and at the net of cobweb dangling from the bulb.

Translucent, tinsel bubbles wobble, slide and plop down the grubby grass. Oxeye daisies, meadowsweet and chervil dribble a duet. Daddy long legs scrambles back and forth ... back and forth ... back and forth ... the final drowsy dollop in a lazy rhythmic dance ...

Through the open door you can see Mr Coyne hunched beside the range, slurping back black tea. His empty eggshell lies discarded with the breadcrumbs on his plate. He looks up, nods in greeting and points with yellow index finger to the doughy bread. You take a slice politely. The tea gushes from the spout. The milk is streamy, creamy.

You move out to the cow shed. Your eyes distinguish four dark bulks, your ears an intermingling snivelling, your nose their steamy sweat. Mr Coyne leaves the door open and the wind reminds of the morning cold outside. A flagstone

177

foreground, manure in the middle, the corner of the red barn and behind, the jagged ridge, robed in prickly gorse and furze. In these unfamiliar minutes of the dawning day, you can well imagine how Bean Draoí an aitinn haunts the hill up there. At first your fingers grope awkwardly, numbly. He has his back to you, but you still feel foolish. Milk pinpricks his bucket in rapid rhythm, then you achieve a squirt, a broken spatter and bubbles in the milk. Only three are spraying, you can't work the fourth teat no matter what. Your back is aching but he says to leave it. Three calves jostle in their stalls. There is a grey one and a black one and a speckled red one. Mr Coyne slops milk from pail to pail. He thrusts two down and you grip the third for the grey one. You like her the best because she doesn't bang and ram her head against the bucket. Her tongue splashes milk on your nose while she slurps and swallows. Mr Coyne slips off his glasses and wipes them. His skin is rippled with wrinkles and criss-crossed blotches of red and blue and purple. He says to stand outside to stop the cows straying into the hen-house, but they turn right and you feel silly waving your arms at their retreating rumps. Mr Coyne prods them onwards now and again. His stick is old and twisted, yours is a smaller replica. A damp drizzle spins in sheets against your cheeks. He turns up his collar; he has a cap and you have a hood. There is lots of mud and puddles because you are taking the long road. The gate is red with rust and is tied with rope. You have to lift it up and push. Raspberry fuschia weaves a wild tapestry with roses, butterwort with clover, rocks with black bog rush. You see his blood, his face, his written words, the birds, his voice, are still asleep, but you see his cross that single stumpy tree. There is the deserted house of stone, still there, alone and crumbling. The tiny window front and back betrays a hidden past, as does the buckled, crumpled land where potato stalks stopped growing. Mr Coyne says you've earned a rest. He sits idly smoking. The cows rasp the grass. Light brightens the Bens, now bound in a ribbon of rainbow. Lakes are a lighter blue, the sea is too. It's going to be a day for the beach, or a day for saving hay, depending on your point of view.

When you get back, everyone is up and talking, shatter-ing the silence, except Cathy of course who never surfaces before midday.

'I heard you getting up for the milking,' yawns Mom.

'It must have been about seven, Michael. Aren't you *starving*? – How is Mr Coyne?'

'The same as always. We went over the second hill. The view was amazing. You could see Kylemore and guess what, I milked the grey cow.'

'That was nice,' she replies vaguely, stifling another yawn.

'Shane, can you hurry up and shave before the bathroom is taken over. I want messages in Moyard: three milk, one brown sliced ...'

'You didn't wake me for the milking Mike. You're mean,' shouts fiery, freckled Jane.

'You can't come. You're too small.'

'Mommy, tell Mike he's to bring me milking tomorrow.'

'Four tomatoes – Don't interrupt Jane – six apples, a brack and see if they have any nice homemade buns.'

'Cathy, can I come in?'

'Go away. I'm still asleep.'

Cathy is sixteen, lazy and bossy. She has a boyfriend, so she thinks she's the bee's knees. Mom says she should read something else apart from Mills and Boon, but Cathy says it's educating her for life. If she gets a new spot, she sulks and asks me for advice, as if I'd know. I don't get spots, but she says to wait 'til I'm older. She tells me secrets sometimes about Kevin, like when they meet at night in the barn. Mom caught her once coming in covered in straw and she read her the riot act. Cathy glared at me and threw her eyes to heav-en, which made Mom even madder. Cathy let on she had been looking for her Claddagh ring, but Mom who has eyes in the back of her head, said what was it doing then in on her dressing table.

'Are the windbreaker and groundsheet in the boot? Michael, count the towels and swimsuits and are the buckets

179

and spades in? Shane, take this picnic basket. Michael, where is your sister Cathy? *Cathy*, if you're not dressed in five minutes, we're going to the beach without you! Shane, that girl is the bane of my life.'

Mom always gets flustered at times like this. Going to the beach is like moving house.

Bathroom door bangs shut, the bolt is drawn back, the toilet flushes; silence, a tap splashes, Cathy storms out – a flimsy glimpse of tousled hair and bedraggled dressing-gown.

Daddy turns the car on the crackling gravel. We tumble in. One missing. 'Go without her,' snorts Mom.

'I'm coming,' screams Cathy. 'Move over!' she orders.

'Ouch! You're squashing me.'

'Stop pinching me, Jane!'

The beach reeks of salty seaweed. You like the slush of spray and the sun in sandhills. Daddy doesn't. He says sand gets in his sandwiches. Crinkled coral litters the strand. You collect it in bags to bring home. Mom's spotted a French family behind rocks without clothes. She says foreigners are disgraceful and should be banned from Irish beaches. The tide is coming in, so you have to swim now and eat later.

The sand is sharp underfoot with razor ribboned shells and barbed brown seaweed. Cold water slaps your ankles. Jane shrieks and runs out. Cathy is brave and does a dog paddle. You stay in too long and come out splashing and shivering, teeth chattering, hair dripping. You wrap up in a warm towel. A good rub and a race and a change of togs. Mom hands you a beaker of scalding tea. Too late – you've burnt your tongue. Cathy is jabbering something nonsensical about her latest patch of freckles. You scowl at her. She drops her mirror.

'*Jane*, what's that awful thing you're holding. It *stinks*.'

Jane triumphantly brandishes a spiky black ball.

'Don't you dare come near me.' Cathy likes melo-dramatics.

'Jane,' snaps Mom, 'leave your sister alone and stop jig-acting with that yoke. Put it back where you found it.'

'That yoke,' says Daddy mildly from behind his newspaper, 'is a sea urchin. If you leave it to dry in the sun, the spikes fall out, and you're left with a hollow pink shell.'

Mom shudders.

'Cathy! *Look!* There's Kevin.'

'Oh my God! Where? Stop pointing Mike. Quick, hide. I'm not here. Mom, I can't let him see me like this.'

'He *has* seen you. He's coming over. Hi Kevin ...'

Rain rustles softly; the final drowsy dollop in a lazy rhythmic dance ...

'Kevin?'

I sit up. The Bens emerge: a pattern of rockstrewn blue, becoming smooth; twelve stark slopes of lemon and lime. I glance at my watch. It's stopped. The hours and minutes and seconds all standing static. Slowly, I wind it on.

The cogs begin to move as time grinds on.

I step outside and close the door on the house of childhood, for I am no longer a child. The wishy-washy wind beats faster. Seagulls cry and dive. Even the bushes swish ten years taller.

Esther

Ursula de Brún

On her way to the check-out, Esther shrugged and threw a fifth can of baked beans into her trolley. What the hell, Esther, she thought, live dangerously. She should be so lucky. The last time Esther had lived dangerously was back in New York when she went for a soda with James Arnold. James was tall. James was blonde. James was all of nine years old. None of the girls wanted him; neither did she. But he singled her out for daily bombardments of paper planes with I LOVE YOU etched in the creases. Mortified, she resisted his dubious charms for weeks. 'No, no,' she would cry, 'I gotta go home and help my mother.' (A blatant lie.) But already, excuses that would run the gamut right up to 'I have a headache' were carving a niche in her female psyche. Then, one day, a fit of devil-may-care overwhelmed her and she went. That reckless, daring feeling never came again; until today.

With a distinct lack of poise, she held on with one hand to the heavy glass door of the supermarket and pushed her trolley out with the other. In the sunshine she shaded her eyes searching for Norm. Norm was the man in her ever predictable life. She knew where she was likely to find him; in the sports shop, talking golf clubs, their offspring whining by his side.

She and Norm had married in a flicker of passion. He had swept her off her feet in a matter of years. Ten to be exact.

'So what are you waiting for?' her mother had railed. 'Norman Feinstein is a good man. You want that Robert Redford should walk through the door?'

No, but she would have settled for Bob Smyth, high school jock extraordinaire.

Once he had asked her for a dime for a phone call and actually smiled at her. In her ecstatic confusion she had handed him a quarter and insisted he keep the change; he did. They never spoke again. Later she heard he married a beauty pageant queen. It figured.

It wasn't that Esther was unhappy with Norm; because she wasn't. He was a kind, loving husband and a patient father, a glorious trait considering the children they had been blessed with. It was just that lately she was out of sorts. She had the feeling that real life was whizzing by in the fast lane while she puttered along in a risk-free zone.

Lately she had wanted to shout 'Will the real Esther Feinstein please stand up!' Betty her best friend hinted darkly at early menopause. Bull, she was thirty-four years old, it was more likely a delayed seven-year itch.

She decided not to fetch Norm and the kids straight away; instead she opted for a few quiet moments in the sun at one of the benches in the little square. Esther would never have announced it at a feminist forum, but she liked shopping centres, especially this one in Dublin.

They had moved to Ireland three years before; Esther very reluctantly. Norm had had no such qualms; Ireland, his company had told him, had wonderful golf courses. Nobody had thought to mention the rain. In the beginning, lonely and frustrated, Esther had revelled in the sight of him, a freezing sodden mass, returning after thirty-six holes. Eventually, they had all settled in, she with new friends and the children happy at school. Then why, three years and another Saturday older, should she imagine she was carrying around a secret person deep inside her? Who was she? Esther wished she knew. She really did.

As she walked along the side of the supermarket, a colourful blob kept pace with her in the glass. A sideways glance told her that her mirror image looked smaller this week. That half pound had made all the difference. Delighted, she sucked in her stomach and realigned her stretch marks.

Struggling around the corner she wished just once she could manage to pick a trolley with a forward disposition. She bumped hers sideways over the decorative cobblestones – guaranteed to crack five out of a dozen eggs – straight into the back of an unsuspecting gentleman. He was, a gentleman that is; not a murmur of reproach as she released the trolley from his heel, a small wince perhaps, but not a murmur.

Apologies flowed effortlessly from her lips. Esther had been apologising for Esther for as long as she could remember; she was a real pro. (Once in broad daylight, she had begged the apologies of a street lamp. The following Monday her mother took her for bifocals.) As she began to back away, she noticed that a large crowd had gathered. They were all staring up in her direction. Self-doubt immediately took hold. Had she streaked the false tan she had put on her legs? Maybe there was egg dripping down through the trolley? She twisted around to check. Her legs were all over bronze, a bit dark perhaps, but no streaks and if the eggs were broken they had opted for maximum concealment; there wasn't a yolk in sight. Then what the hell were they all staring at?

A trumpet blast in her right ear answered her. She had been so intent on the damage she'd inflicted on the nice man that she hadn't noticed that he was accompanied by five others, all identically dressed in white shirts, dark pants and red waistcoats. It was a jazz band. The shopping centre traders were having one of their 'entertain the customers' afternoons.

Thrilled, Esther excused herself all the way over to the side. To say she liked jazz was to make the understatement of the year. You might as well say cows like grass. It was her greatest passion; Norm didn't even come close. She would have liked to have shared it with him but, as with everything else, Norm was middle-of-the-road. Give him Barry Manilow or Neil Diamond and he was musically sated.

'Neil Schmeil,' she would say as he lay on the couch enraptured with 'Song Sung Blue'. 'Give me Ella Fitzgerald any day.'

She knew Ella's repertoire better than the names of her own children. No sooner would Norm leave for the office and the kids for school when Ella would spin on the turntable and Esther would clean the house in a blissful duet as she made her way out of the living-room and up the stairs with the vacuum cleaner. And now, here she was with a few peaceful moments to herself, listening to a band playing all her favourite numbers.

If the essence of good comedy is 'timing' perhaps that's why her life felt like such a joke. She was born in the wrong decade. By a cruel twist of fate she had missed the 1940s. She was out of synch. Even today's clothes didn't suit her. With a sigh, she closed her eyes, she forgot Norm, she forgot the kids and gave herself over to the music, body swaying, foot tapping.

'Blue skies ...' the singer sang, '... nothing but blue skies.'

Her favourite fantasy rushed to the surface. It was the big band era and Duke Ellington was on stage. He was introducing a singer, no, not Ella, Esther. Esther Romero (not even in fantasy could she use Feinstein). She swept gracefully to centre stage, cool and confident as she took her place before the mike. Within seconds she had seduced the audience crooning 'A Russian Lullaby'. A low bow. Rapturous applause.

Esther had never told a soul, but all she ever wanted to do was sing with a big band, live a life of glamour and above all, be famous. But she never did anything about it. All her auditions, performances and beautifully executed bows had taken place before her bedroom mirror; her microphone a tin of hairspray. She opened her eyes. The music had stopped and her reverie was broken. The lead singer was speaking and she had missed his first few words.

'What did he say?' she asked a woman beside her.

'He asked if anyone would like to come up and sing. He must be joking. Nobody'd have the nerve.'

Esther nodded but her heart was beginning to thump heavily in her chest and her hands tightly clenched the handle of the trolley. No Esther, absolutely not, she said to herself. You couldn't. You wouldn't. Not here. Would you? What would Norm say? What would your mother say? My mother? How did she get into this?

The force of her inner debate was such that she thought she had spoken aloud. But nobody was giving her funny looks and the band had launched into 'I'm Putting All My

Eggs Into One Basket'. She sure was; she should be at home scrambling them. Esther turn your trolley around, go directly to the sports shop, do not pass go, do not collect ... she couldn't move, the feeling was too strong.

Norm, where are you when I need you? I'm about to do something crazy, she cried to herself, as she propelled her trolley towards the band. She approached the lead singer. He recoiled in memory of their first meeting.

'I'd like to sing with the band.' There. The words were out.

'Great,' he smiled wickedly. 'What do you know? The "Trolley Song"?'

Esther wasn't impressed. Her lips were trembling and her tongue had stuck to the roof of her mouth.

'Anything by Irving Berlin,' she croaked, her face the colour of scalded beetroot.

They had finished their number and she was being announced: 'Ladies and gentlemen, we have a young lady here ...'

Did he say young? Eat your heart out Betty, she grinned. The man continued.

' ... her name is ...?' He looked down at her.

'Esther, eh, just Esther,' she replied. No point in over-doing it, there might be a neighbour in the crowd.

'Her name, ladies and gentlemen is Esther. What key do you sing in Esther?'

She stared blankly at him. Key? She had never needed a key. Ella had always looked after that end of things. She recovered herself.

'The same key as Ella Fitzgerald sings in. I'll sing "I Used to be Colourblind", if you know it.'

He handed her a mike. 'Great stuff,' he said. Then he was counting them in. 'A one, a two, a three ...'

The mike was heavier than the hairspray, she needed a drink of water, her legs wobbled, she stared down at her toes, why hadn't she put on fresh nail polish? Where was the glittering dress, the velvet-curtained back-drop? She opened her mouth. Please God, let something out.

'Strange, how a dreary world can suddenly change ...'

186

She was singing, her voice was fine. Now all she had to do was take her chin out of her chest.

' ... To a world as bright as the evening star ...'

Her audience were not sitting elegantly dressed, sipping champagne; they were standing around in jeans and eating ice cream. But they were smiling; they liked her. Project, Esther, project!

' ... Queer what a difference when your vision is clear ...'
She felt light. She felt free. She let them have it!

' ... And you see things as they really are ...'

'Hey, that's Mom!' a voice shouted from the crowd. She smiled down at her dumbstruck husband and excited children.

' ... I used to be colourblind but I met you and now I find there's green in the grass, there's gold in the moon, there's blue in the skies ...'

The real Esther Feinstein had finally stood up.

Nothing Changes Except the Water

Peter Hutchinson

Dear Sis,

Greetings from the Middle East!

Anthony is doing me a great service by leaving this message for you at the Theatre because he's also delivering a letter to our Mother. I don't want you to show her this note, she has enough on her plate, what with Dad gone and me so far away and everything.

I know that I should have written sooner but we have moved around so much there wasn't much time.

How are things with you? The story before I left was that your group was reviving Terence's half dozen plays. Haven't much regard, myself, for works that are surely rather ordinary. Don't go all defensive, now, who am I to judge the quality of plays, eh? Anyway, best of luck with 'em.

I'd have thought, though, that you'd be more interested in the dance, that's all. What a waste of grace and beauty, standing around, declaiming with perfect diction lines of appalling mediocrity. Still, if that's your bag. But someone like yourself would surely be tempted to disport yourself if you saw some of the native dancers here. They bewilder men. Arms and legs and curving body movements are only incidental to the swirling veils and the invitation in their eyes. Generations of gypsies in the blood, that must be it. On second thoughts, how could a nice refined and civilised girl like my sister ever get herself involved in such unrestrained behaviour.

Only teasing, Sis, only teasing. An actress can simulate anything, can't she? Perhaps that's why I'm putting so much trust in you. I'll explain later on.

For a start, I'll plunge ahead with the bad news. I'm writing this really to let you know that the whole country of Lebanon is acting up again. Some pun, eh, with you in the theatre business? I'm on detachment further south as you can see but I expect to be recalled north soon as hardly a day goes by without disturbing reports involving our forces. Several of our lads have disappeared, kidnapped we believe and our officers are getting very edgy. HQ blames them for slack security and as a result they often take it out on us in the ranks.

Even as far south as this outpost the effect of guerrilla tactics miles away is beginning to wear us down. We tend to herd together at night. Very few of us get midnight passes unless we undertake to travel in pairs.

I don't know what will come out of all this unrest. Now and then we hear of efforts at peace negotiations but against that the rumour-mongers from surrounding villages whisper of new leaders emerging from among the native population, men who are dissatisfied with the way their masters are behaving.

There's even talk of a general uprising.

All this is leading up to what I want to say to you, Sis. I don't know what's going to happen out here. It all may end happily but just in case, try to stay close to our Mother, keep up a good front and don't let her get despondent if any bad news breaks at home. She needs you now, Sis, now that there are no men in the house. You might even bring some eligible bachelor home! How about that?

I know that I can trust you to put a good face on things. D'you remember the day you nicked all of my weekly allowance and then against all my accusations you persuaded Dad to buy me a good strong leather purse? You were a great actress even then. No bother to you.

And what's more, in spite of everything I'm still
Your loving brother.

P.S. Burn this, and pretend that the letter to Mother and yourself is the only one.

189

Dear Mum and Sis,

I know that you were sad at the time when I told you that I
intended to join up. But really, what choice did I have? No
work and no prospect of work. You know me and so you
must have known that I had no intention of walking the
streets or standing at corners.

I must confess that I had misgivings myself but if you
were to see me now you'd be pleasantly surprised. Honestly!
My tunic fits me very well, with no sign of a bulge at the
middle. In fact I've had to pull in my belt a couple of notches
since my first day in training. You'd really be proud of me!

But all that is not the reason for this letter, pleasant
though that news is. You will already have noticed of course
that I'm writing from abroad. Now, Mum, don't get all upset. As I've said, when I left home there was only one place
that I could go. And don't you remember that Dad used to
say to me, 'Wherever you make your bed, boy, there you
must lie on it'? Well, it was the army for me and wherever it
sends me, there I'll willingly go. Would I be my father's son
otherwise?

You miss Dad, Mum, I know that. But when you plead-
ed with me not to join up was it not perhaps Dad's death
clouded your mind and made you think that poisoned
arrows were waiting for every soldier on a foreign field?
Believe me, it's just not like that. And anyway, didn't somebody say somewhere that there was more danger in the
home than on the road? Please smile now, Mum, and don't
be angry, all right?

When our company commander paraded us and told us
that we were detailed for foreign service I didn't have time
to get word to you before we left barracks. No, that's not
true. I could have applied for a few days leave. But don't
you see how strained those days would have been? I
couldn't face you, Mum.

I kept busy. We had to draw field rations for the journey.
The quartermaster issued us with special headgear and
footwear and each of us had to sign for modern weapons –

190

purely for defensive purposes you understand. You mustn't imagine that we were going to the Middle East to wage war. It was nothing like that. Our orders were that we were simply to keep our wits about us, try to maintain friendly relations with the native population, but not to get too friendly with the local girls!

Well, we've been here some time now and things are rather quiet. It's fair to say, though, that we are not wanted in this country. Very few of the people even greet us civilly. I suppose it's hard to blame them. We do have to put up occasional checkpoints and this is bound to cause delay and frustration. And then there's the search for concealed weapons. One doesn't have to be too sensitive to imagine the degradation they feel at being searched by foreigners. Apart from those unpleasant duties, life goes on peacefully enough.

I miss you and I know that you miss me, but roll on the time when my tour of duty is over. I'll be back home with you and we'll be able to laugh together at all the tales I have to tell you about this foreign station.

There is one hardship, though. I wouldn't want you to see my hair just now, now that the company hair-cutter has been to work on me. How I look forward, Mum, to the gentle touch of your hands and the loving way you used to arrange my curls. YOU never trimmed my thatch to the very bone!

Honestly I hope no one else gets to read this. Please don't show it to anyone else. You must know how proud I am of my military prowess and I made Anthony, my mate in the company we relieved, I made him swear not to unseal this letter bringing it to you. As for putting it through the regular channels!!

You must be wondering how I spend my time when I'm not on duty. Well, I stay in camp most of the time and when we're not competing in various outdoor games, we shoot dice for small bets. Throwing dice can be an art in itself but of course gambling for high stakes is forbidden. We dice mainly at night by the light of our lanterns and we usually post sentries discreetly because I needn't tell you, sometimes

191

the stakes do rise a bit. But enough of that.

You'll be glad to learn that I'm quite good at track sports. We use the perimeter of the camp and if I say so myself, I am seldom out of the first three home. Some of my mates mock me and say that if danger ever comes I'll be the longest distance away from it and in the shortest time. I wouldn't disagree. I'm no hero. I hold, however, that to be good at athletics is to be in line for promotion. Just look at all the people who have become famous because of their superiority at sports.

As I've already mentioned, Anthony's company is going home hence this letter. But in addition to the official warnings about mixing with the locals I learned from him that it is unwise and in fact foolhardy to fall in love with any of the women here. Does that make you happy now? Adultery is a pretty serious crime over here, not that I have any plans in that direction, ha-ha, and also of course we are not subject to their laws.

It would be impossible for an ordinary soldier like me to describe all the various political movements in this country. I understand that it is even more complicated in Lebanon where most of our troops are stationed but I can tell you that in our particular sector there is no end to the number of roving bands of malcontents who would like to see us out of here. But as I've said, we've been sent to keep the peace and keep it we will.

I don't know for certain how long we'll be kept here. It all depends on the local situation. From what I can gather, if it looks as if the native authorities are capable of maintaining law and order for the foreseeable future, then we will be withdrawn to a central strongpoint from where we can be dispatched at first signs of trouble; IF there is any trouble, which is unlikely. And don't forget, no one runs better or faster than I can!

So don't be worried, Mum. And before I close, let me show you that the story is not all doom and gloom. After first parade the other day I was detailed for duty at a local wedding. How about that! 'Twas just to make sure no unruly elements showed up, so for the duration of the celebration I was the official patrol. Why me, you ask with furrowed brow? Well, you must be aware of my natural charm!!! But wasn't it a good sign of co-operation between ourselves and at least some of the locals? Apparently a few out-of-town dignitaries were invited and the father of the bride wanted to make a good impression.

Naturally I had to keep a prudent distance from the merrymaking, being a stranger and a foreign one at that but well, I had an enjoyable day of it away from camp chores, and guard duty always under a blazing sun.

I had plenty to eat and I was free to stroll around on the outskirts of the house. I kept strictly sober of course but as the day drew to a close I gave the high sign to one of the servants that I'd appreciate a drop of liquid sustenance.

I saw him approach the chief steward who soon came across to me with a large jug of wine held carefully in his hands. I drank thirstily, found the wine to be superb and asked him was it from a local vineyard. He smiled in a puzzled way and replied: 'People generally serve the best wine first but this bridegroom has kept the best wine till now.'

How right he was.

I must say that I'll be kind of sorry to leave this outpost of Cana in Galilee.

I love you both. Look after yourselves until I return to Rome.

MARCUS

The Coast of Malabar

John Maher

He sits, gap-toothed and grinning. Eyes upon all about him. Lips tainted with bitter retorts. An old man now, John. Seedless belly. Short measure dealt for all. He grins again, then angles himself before his circle of listeners. Like a death's head beckoning in malice. Smiling, his listeners crowd about him. They hear John tell again the tale of the man, the woman and the sojourner.

'Dillon and her. There he is now. Over in the corner. Well, speak of the devil! They both shacked up together in a small flat off the Broadway. Oh, they were like that for a few years. All grand and easy. Before she took ill, that was.'

It is morning. They wake as one. Dull light of a winter's morning tilting at their senses once more. Dillon lays his hand upon her head. They speak softly over breakfast, then part. He drives off to his employment bureau. A taskmaster. Days spent talking with those who are passing through. Short-term jobs. She, Ann, takes the train to a Polytech. Colours on cloth. Waxed images. In the evening they meet again. They seldom go out at night. They sit and read. They talk. She sketches. Sometimes the phone rings. Dillon is brief and direct when he speaks to the unseen voices. At times, lifting his head from the 'paper, he watches her as she walks towards the kitchen or turns to fetch something. He wonders how it would feel to have her presence taken away from him. He damns the notion as soon as he notes its pull.

The listeners take their ease at a moment. The older man puts his hand into his pocket. He calls for another round. John. He picks at his teeth with a matchstick. Winks towards his audience. Someone nods at him. At John. Old sag-bellied teller of tales. Quietly begrudging of the lives about him. He will talk on about the man, the woman and the stranger. The others listen, smiling his careful smile.

'Whatever it was, she came down very sudden with it. Galloping consumption. Nice names for the other, I suppose. You'd never be told anyway. He tried to nurse her himself, you see. Spent half the day looking after her. Neglected the business of course. Spent every penny he had on the best treatment available. That was the sort of him. Anyway, she was past help. She was already gone too far by the time the illness was discovered. Do you follow me?'

It is morning. Dillon hears her as she tries to stifle a cough. He returns to the bedroom in haste. She fixes her gaze upon the book in her hands. Sitting on the edge of the bed, he lays his hand upon her head.

'I can stay for the day. It's no problem.'

'No, you won't. It's all right again now.'

'Are you sure?'

Alone, he wanders about the kitchen, affecting to tidy things away. He delays in order to hear if she will cough again. He wonders now, at what will happen to him when her presence is drawn away. A coldness comes upon his thoughts.

John, grown goutish and arrogant in his years. The listeners disperse for a moment, to watch a tall man pot a pool ball. They return again. He gathers them about him, waiting until they have all been baited by his silence. Then he leans forward once more. The callous grin of the careful storyteller. He beckons to them. The white shirt, the stout frame. A bloated smile. John tells on, of the man, of the woman and of the stranger.

Just after Christmas it was. The worst time of the year you could pick. She went very quickly. Don't ask me whether she was in pain or not. I suppose they had her on some kind of dope towards the end. Brompton cocktail. Isn't that what they call it? He lost his reason. Before she was even buried. We used to see him in here. He took it very bad. Broke up completely, he was. Became very hard on himself. Wouldn't speak to anyone. Hadn't a civil word for his own friends even. He stayed that way for a long time. He went back home for the funeral, you see. That was the real mistake. To set foot back home at all. Why couldn't he leave well enough alone? A very thick-headed man, Dillon.

Rains cutting in swathes across a grey churchyard. Dillon stands at a distance from the dead girl's family. Red-cheeked mother by the gaping grave. Salt spray on wind-blushed skin. The father. Thin reed of a soft-tempered man. His sons and daughters refusing, as one, to glance back towards the intruder standing silently by the stile. This was all then: a train journey back to Dublin after the funeral. A boat across the sea. Then, the first evening alone in the apartment. Sitting, crying in his cups. Falling to sleep without relief. The evenings without number after that. Sounds coming from other rooms. He would turn, startled, then read her absence once again in the bitter silence. Slowly, the heart hardening as the months passed. Drifting back to that out of which he had so recently come. Emigrants in gloomy pubs. Their weekend haunts. Brash talk and heavy drinking. The coldness of his words telling those who knew him of the dying of the heart.

Hang-jowl John, eager now to continue the tale, carries on. The listeners, half-dozing before his words. Of the woman who died, of the man. Of the stranger who called one day. He moves his chair in towards the table. Elbow on the damp surface. Jabs with his finger. He calls his bearers closer. Gap-toothed smile to damn all about him.

'He turned in on himself after that. Then he went wild again. He'd be out 'til all hours of the night. Big red eyes on him. You'd see him in here often – over there in the corner by the phone. He'd be sitting there, as true as Jesus, chatting away to himself. Nobody paying a blind bit of attention to him at all. A thing which went against his business in the end. I believe he became so crooked in himself that he went and gave some big donation to some sort of political appeal or other. They saw him coming. I think to myself, that he would have lashed out at anybody in the state he was in at the time. It all seemed to come to a halt a short while after this chap turned up on his doorstep. Looking for a start he was. Anywhere. A stranger. Took Dillon out of himself a bit. Gave him somebody to worry about besides himself. And he did his best for the chap. Fed him and clothed him too, from what I hear. Sorted him out with a soft number, up in Harlesden. There are three sorts they say you should never begrudge your company to. A widow, a blind man and a stranger. A bird of passage. And that's what the chap was. Only a bird of passage. But Dillon didn't see that. Or maybe he didn't want to see that. Sure he almost adopted the chap. More fool he.'

Dillon sits in his office. There is a young man before him. A stranger, with a quiet and watchful manner about him. Dillon sees a young man, soft tongued and straight from the boat. The stranger sees a middle-aged man, strangely uneasy for his years. After sorting out an interview for the stranger, Dillon stands up to put on his coat. He taps his watch.

'I want you back here by eleven tomorrow. Right?'

'I'll be here on the dot.'

'Where did you get my name from, if it's no harm to ask?'

'Below in the Cock. Last night.'

'Steer clear of that kip, will you. Rough lot. All talk merchants.'

'I will.'

'Eleven tomorrow, horse. For the cards and the rest of it. Good luck.'

The following morning, having arranged for registration with a friend at the exchange, Dillon drives the young man back to his own flat. He gives him a clean shirt to wear for the interview. They sit together over coffee. The younger man looks about the flat. Bookcases. Potted plants, ceramics. Prints. Kandinsky. Batiks. Dillon notes the eyes which measure all.

'I live here on my own. Since my girlfriend died.'

197

'Oh ...'

'Most of that stuff up there belonged to her. Prints. That kind of thing. I wouldn't bother my arse throwing it out.'

'I know what you mean.'

He drops the young man by the tube station, allowing him find his own way to the interview. Then he turns back for the bureau once more.

Someone had taken the stage. He sits before the piano. It is evening now. John gives grudging ear to the songs. Sometimes he talks over the music, drawing his company away from the familiar words and the melodies well-worn. The number about him has dwindled to a pair of young labourers and a stray who had chanced in with them. Dillon has taken a seat at the next table. John, his tongue idling a moment, turns his back on the rough-haired man at the piano who sings an odd, jaunty Cockney song.

'Where was it I was? Ah, yes. Well, anyway, he took the young lad in. Bed, board and all. It was the company he was after you see. A funny thing that, you might say. To take a complete stranger in under your roof. Never mind if it was one of your own. They spent a lot of time together too. They used go out to things. He stopped chasing his tail around the pubs, anyway. The young lad got a chance to find his feet over here. It was six of one. There was nothing unnatural about the business, if you see what I'm driving at. They were just company for one another. That was all.'

It is evening. Rain bears down upon the city outside. Dillon sits by the dull light of the table lamp, scouring the morning paper. In the kitchen, the young man sits writing a letter. There is a print hanging on the wall behind him; a man leaning over a gate, watching the progress of the seasons. Smiling, a dark man. Autumn in one corner of the field; spring at the opposite end. In the gap between, the callous sun of high summer giving onto the cold, cramped earth of winter. Dillon calls from his newspaper. Later on, they drive down to the Broadway and take the late hour in a noisy bar. They have spoken at length over the months. The younger man has learned to listen without question as he sips his drink. Dillon speaks of the woman's decline. The younger man listens, bearing the undertones of bitterness with patience. Slowly, Dillon comes around to mentioning her by name. Uneasily, at first, he tags tales onto his memories of her. When he plays cards, he sometimes looks away from his companions as her name starts to drift across his tongue. Then, one day as they sit together at evening, he speaks his sadness to the younger man.

'Is it worth all the trouble? Never again, boy. No, James. Never again. I couldn't take it twice.'

The singer steps down from the podium to take a rest. The crowded bar falls back into smaller groups again. John, sag-bellied and saw-toothed, leans across the table towards the two labourers. The man at the next table does not hear. He is lost to those about him. He muses to himself as one in pursuit of some secret melody. John hunches up his shoulders and, glancing at the silent one at the next table, continues. His lips are set in an attitude both of distaste and mockery He rubs his stubbled chin and winks at the two labourers. He snaps his fingers.

'And then, just like that, the young chap is gone again. Not a trace. Just when Dillon was starting to pull himself together. There's gratitude for you. He fed him, he clothed him. And the young chap goes and does a moonlight without as much as a word of thanks. The little get! And what did Dillon think of it all? Will you riddle me that, says the fellow. Anyway, I heard a long time after, that the cute little bollix had took off back home with some quare one. There's love for you. Love you and leave you!'

It is a cold, damp morning and an evil sky sits over the city. Dillon stumbles from his bedroom and calls the young man for work. There is no answer. He calls again, then knocks slowly on the bedroom door. There is no one within. Turn-

199

ing on the light in the kitchen, he sees the note lying on the table. He recognises the handwriting, but will not read the message. He casts the milk bottle he holds onto the cold, tiled floor. When he finally leaves the flat for the office, he will take his humour from the sky above and his comfort from the misery of those about him.

They are calling out his name now.

'John! John! Give us a bar of a song there!'

Gap-toothed, he smiles at their number. The two labourers bang their pint glasses off the table. To one side the dark man, Dillon, watches as John in his frayed suit ascends the stage. Through eyes heavy with the evening's drink. He leans back in his chair as the labourers quit their clamouring. John looks down from the podium.

'All right. I'll give ye one so. You won't be able to say I wouldn't oblige. A sad one. I like the sad ones best. I think you have probably all heard me sing it before now.'

He clears his throat and glances back towards the piano.

Far away across the ocean
Underneath an Indian star
Dwelt a lovely dark-eyed maiden
On the coast of Malabar.

The pianist moved his hands over the keys. Slowly, he threads the sullen tune onto the words he hears. Dillon shifts in his chair and looks up at the figure on the podium. Words threading thoughts threading words. When first I foot set in this city. Rooming houses and sweat of man. Men who must spend the rest of their days before the shovel. Then leaving these behind for an office. To mix with the sort who worked the men who worked the shovel. An office and a name. Two rooms on the Broadway. Girl typing in the next room. An apartment. And you, soft Ann. And why, then, suddenly this?

She would raise her lovely dark eyes
And point across the bay
And whisper 'if you love me
Why do you sail away?'

John, swaying as he sings. Someone at the bar turns back to his drink. The two labourers at the next table watch Dillon. They see his eyes drift from sense and sound. A cry once, he, Dillon, heard. On the bare night, once. Room in a big house. Storm over Kilburn. Chinese girl. Keening to herself and wailing the whole night through. Soul-lost sound. Hearing the following morning that her child had died the previous day. Like print on the wall in the flat. Ann's print. James who explained it first. Walked by it a thousand times and never looked. Four panels, I think. Yes. In the corner, a skeleton dressed in top hat and tails with a big smirk on his puss. Watching the seasons pass in turn. Why did they take you? What did I not do?

> I can see that crowded city
> With its palm trees green and tall
> And the starry night she danced with me
> Inside the city hall.

Someone calls from the crowd.

'Come on, John! Good man, Kearney!'

The two labourers bang their glasses off the table. The singer looks down at Dillon. Eyes fixed on the floor. Glass held awkwardly in hand, set to fall. Lights dimming all about. Time! A bell ringing. All is gone, I know. A wife once, then sort of son. You both. I will go no more to love you. And then, what is there? Him, smiling by the gate. This, there on the table. And you, John, up on the stage. I see you all right, you bull-nosed bastard. Smiling by the gate. Watching all the seasons pass. Never chance your crooked heart for anything. If it were to happen a thousand times again. Not like you I would be. A thousand times. Rather than you. A thousand times.

> Fare thee well my lovely dark eyes
> Fare thee well my Indian star
> For I'll go no more and love you
> On the coast of Malabar.

The bell is ringing now and there are hands sounding applause. John, teller of the tale, gap-toothed and grinning, is smiling from the podium. Before him, the two labourers sit, sated with the story. One nods to the other and they call to the man at the microphone as they stand up to leave. And there is talk and chatter all around and words left unrequited in each ear. And there is the dark man, alone at his table. Memory stilled for another evening. Water settling once more over a chance pebble cast into a stagnant pool. Dillon, senseless by three empty chairs.

More Mercier Books

THE RED-HAIRED WOMAN
and Other Stories

Sigerson Clifford

'He blamed Red Ellie for his failure to sell. She stood before him on the road that morning, shook her splendid mane of foxy hair at him, and laughed. He should have returned to his house straightaway and waited 'till she left the road. It was what the fishermen always did when they met her. It meant bad luck to meet a red-haired woman when you went fishing or selling. Everyone knew that ...'

'This collection of stories has humour, shrewd observation, sharp wit at times, and the calm sure touch of an accomplished storyteller ... '

FROM THE INTRODUCTION BY BRENDAN KENNELLY.

Each of 'Sigerson Clifford's delicious tales ... in *The Red-Haired Woman and Other Stories* is a quick, often profound glimpse of Irish life, mostly in the countryside. The characters appear, fall into a bit of trouble and get wherever they're going without a lot of palaver. The simple plots glisten with semi-precious gems of language ...'

JAMES F. CLARITY, *THE NEW YORK TIMES BOOK REVIEW*

'Flavoured by the wit and sweetness of the Irish language, this slender volume presents brief affectionate glimpses of Irish country life.'

LEONE MCDERMOTT, *BOOKLIST*

STORIES FROM THE GREAT IRISH WRITERS

Selected by John McCarthy

The Irish are great storytellers and most literary critics rate Irish short story writers as among the best in the world.

Stories from the Great Irish Writers is a collection of beautifully written stories portraying the lighter side of Irish life. From James Joyce to Frank O'Connor you will find the greatest short story writers of all time in this book:

The Party by Frank O'Connor
The Gold in the Sea by Brian Friel
The Scoop by James Plunkett
The Martyr's Crown by Flann O'Brien
Poisson d'Avril by Somerville & Ross
Her Trademark by Julia O'Faolain
The Priest's Housekeeper by Michael McLaverty
A Letter to Rome by George Moore
Exile's Return by Bryan MacMahon
The Can with the Diamond Notch by Seamus O'Kelly
The Anticlerical Pup by Hugh Leonard
The Boarding House by James Joyce
A Voice From the Dead (A Monologue) by Mary Lavin
A Rest and a Change by Honor Tracy
Death in Jerusalem by William Trevor
A Journey to the Seven Streams by Benedict Kiely
"They Also Serve ..." by Mervyn Wall
The Stolen Ass by Liam O'Flaherty
The Fur Coat by Seán O'Faolain
The Last of Mrs Murphy by Brendan Behan

DURANGO

John B. Keane

*Danny Binge peered into the distance and slowly spelled out
the letters inscribed on the great sign in glaring red capitals:*
   'DURANGO,' he read.
   *'That is our destination,' the Rector informed his friend.
'I'm well known here. These people are my friends and before
the night is over they shall be your friends too.'*

The friends in question are the Carabim girls: Dell, aged
seventy-one and her younger sister, seventy-year-old Lily.
Generous, impulsive and warm-hearted, they wine, dine and
entertain able-bodied country boys free of charge – they will
have nothing to do with the young men of the town or indeed any town ...

Durango is an adventure story about life in rural Ireland
during the Second World War. It is a story set in an Ireland
that is fast dying but John B. Keane, with his wonderful skill
and humour, brings it to life, rekindling in the reader
memories of a time never to be quite forgotten ...

IRISH SHORT STORIES

John B. Keane

There are more shades to John B. Keane's humour than there
are colours in the rainbow. Wit, pathos, compassion,
shrewdness and a glorious sense of fun and roguery are seen
in this book. This fascinating exploration of the striking yet
intangible Irish characteristics show us Keane's sensitivity
and deep understanding of everyday life in a rural community.

The Contractors

John B. Keane

The Contractors is a stirring story of people who were forced to emigrate and work in England in the early 1950s. Before leaving Ireland they were warned about the likely evils that they would confront in that pagan place. John B. Keane, with his wonderful skill and humour, brings them to life in these unforgettable pages as he gives us the fascinating details of their daily existence, their exhilarations and their sorrows.

Islanders

Peadar O'Donnell

This powerful novel depicts the life of a small island community off the Donegal coast. It is a story of epic simplicity, of people who confront in their daily lives, hunger, poverty and death by drowing.

Favourite Irish Stories

Selected by Anthony Bluett

Favourite Irish Stories, published to mark the fiftieth anniversary of Mercier Press, brings together many figures including Francis MacManus, Padraic Pearse, Daniel Corkery, John B. Keane, Eric Cross and Eamon Kelly.

All in all, an absorbing and entertaining collection of stories, representative of what Mercier has put into print over the last half-century.

Between Innocence and Peace
Favourite Poems of Ireland

Chosen and Introduced by
Brendan Kennelly

Brendan Kennelly has chosen poems that give him a thrill or a laugh, poems that sing clouds or sunlight into his heart, poems that he is glad to read again and again for a whole host of reasons.

They are all here: sad poems, mad poems, funny poems, lonely poems, poems that demonstrate and celebrate the partitioned culture of Ireland, poems by and about women, poems that tell lies beautifully and truth clumsily, poems that sing the pains and joys of history, that tell of spiritual desolation, physical desire, remorse, love, myth, exile, homesickness, hatred, dreams, prejudice, nightmares, superstition, illness, health, war, religion, disaster and death. And all, all between innocence and peace.

Favourite Poems
We Learned in School

Chosen and Introduced by Thomas Walsh

Thomas Walsh has put together a collection of the most quoted and most memorable poems we learned in school. Most of the poems are by Irish authors, and have a distinctive Irish flavour and one theme in common – they are evocative, the stir a nostalgic chord, and they bring us back to what many see as a better life.

MY VILLAGE – MY WORLD

John M. Feehan

This is a book that never palls or drags. It is boisterous and ribald and I am tempted to say that it is by far the funniest book I have ever read. It is also an accurate and revealing history of rural Ireland half a century ago and more. John M. Feehan writes beautifully throughout. I love this book.

FROM THE FOREWORD BY JOHN B. KEANE

My Village – My World is a fascinating account of ordinary people in the countryside. It depicts a way of life that took thousands of years to evolve and mature and was destroyed in a single generation. As John M. Feehan says 'Nobody famous ever came from our village. None of its inhabitants ever achieved great public acclaim ... The people of our village could be described in government statistics as un-skilled. That would be a false description. They were all highly skilled, whether in constructing privies or making coffins, digging drains or cutting hedges, droving cattle or tending to stallions ... I do not want to paint a picture of an idyllic village like Goldsmith's phony one. We had our sinners as well as our saints ...'

Isle of the Blest

Jerome Kiely

Told in the voice of one who arrived as a stranger to an island but was immediately accepted as a vital part of the close-knit community, *Isle of the Blest* is a beautifully written, timeless evocation of a place and a people apart.